Marilyn Halvorson

As a child, Marilyn Halvorson loved to read books about the Wild West and life on a ranch. When she was just twelve, she received a typewriter for Christmas and began to write stories. Today, she is the author of several award-winning books for young adults, all set in Western Canada. *Cowboys Don't Cry* won the Clarke-Irwin-Alberta Culture Writing for Youth Competition in 1983 and was made into a popular television movie.

A keen observer of relationships, Ms. Halvorson draws heavily on her experiences as a teacher for ideas.

BY THE SAME AUTHOR

Let It Go

Nobody Said It Would Be Easy

Dare

Brothers and Strangers

Stranger on the Run

*To Everything a Season:
A Year in Alberta Ranch Country*

Cowboys Don't Cry

COWBOYS DON'T QUIT

MARILYN HALVORSON

A GEMINI BOOK

Published in 1994 by
Stoddart Publishing Co. Limited
34 Lesmill Road
Toronto, Canada
M3B 2T6
Tel. (416) 445-3333
Fax. (416) 445-5967

Second printing February 1996

Canadian Cataloguing in Publication Data

Halvorson, Marilyn, 1948–
Cowboys don't quit

"Gemini young adult"
ISBN: 0-7736-7425-X

I. Title.

PS8565.A48C69 1994   jC813'.54   C94-931333-5
PZ7.H35Co 1994

Cover Design: Brant Cowie/ArtPlus Limited
Cover Illustration: Albert Slark
Typesetting: Tony Gordon Ltd.

Printed and bound in Canada

*Stoddart Publishing gratefully acknowledges
the support of the Canada Council, the
Ontario Ministry of Citizenship, Culture and Recreation,
Ontario Arts Council, and Ontario Publishing Centre in the
development of writing and publishing in Canada.*

To Dean,
who is definitely
not a quitter

Chapter 1

Dad should be back today. No, I might as well quit lying to myself. He should have been back two days ago.

I kept pushing that thought to the bottom of my mind but just like a spider slipping down the side of a tub, it kept pushing its way back up again. And all these thoughts sure weren't helping me write this killer grade nine math final. 2x minus 2y equals . . .

The truck had broken down. That must be it. Dad would be home as soon as he could get it fixed. Yeah? Then why hadn't he phoned?

2x minus 2y equals 2z. I tried the question for the third time and got a third different answer. Oh, well. The question was multiple guess anyway. When all else fails, pick C. Besides, C was Casey Sutherland's initial.

I glanced over two rows to where Casey was sitting, hoping she'd look up and smile. But naturally *she* was concentrating on the exam. I sighed and tried the next question.

Half an hour later I scrawled my name on the top of my paper, tossed it onto the growing pile on Mr. Crandall's desk, and escaped into the June sunshine. Math was our last exam, but the buses didn't leave till noon so I hung around killing time with the rest of the country kids.

Casey finally came out to lean on the sun-hot wall beside me. "So," she said with a grin, "what'd you think?"

I rolled my eyes. "Well, I'll say one thing for Crandall. He's consistent. His exam didn't make any more sense than his classes did."

Casey laughed and tossed her hair back. "Come on, Shane, it wasn't *that* bad. There's the bus. Race you!"

We charged for the bus and landed, out of breath, in the back seat that was usually claimed by a couple of high school kids who'd finished exams last week. "You had a head start," I said accusingly. "Sure, Shane," Casey laughed, and then gave me a puzzled look. "What are you doing?"

"What I've been wantin' to do for ten months." I

was tearing up my math notes, page by page. Goodbye exponents. So long geometry. Au revoir binomials.

"You are warped, Shane Morgan."

I grinned. "Yup. But at least I'm happily warped. So, what are you gonna do this afternoon?"

"I don't know. Guess I'll see if Mom needs any help in the clinic. Want to come up and see if she's got any interesting new patients?"

I hesitated. Any other time I would have gone. Casey's mom was a vet and she had her clinic right on their ranch, next door to our place. It's interesting there. I hang around a lot, and even get paid for the work I do on weekends. But I didn't want to go to the clinic today. Right now I had just one thing on my mind. When the bus came over the hill above our house the first thing I'd see was Dad's truck parked in the yard. He and I had a whole lot of catching up to do.

I shook my head. "Not today, Case."

Casey said something but I missed it because the bus had just topped the hill. I looked down at our yard, below. Everything was the same as always — the house and barn, the grove of spruce trees, the horses grazing in the pasture, the old Ford half-ton — everything but the four-by-four and trailer that Dad had driven off to Montana last week.

Something that felt like a big rock settled into the pit of my stomach. He was supposed to be gone for four days. Tomorrow morning would make it six. Even for Dad that was too much of a difference. Unless . . .

"Shane?" Casey's voice brought me back.

"Huh?"

"I just asked if you'd heard anything from your dad. Shouldn't he be back by now?"

I swung around in the seat to face her. "What are you so worried about? Dad knows what he's doin'. If he's a couple days late it's nobody's business but his own."

Casey's eyes widened and she sort of pulled back in the seat like I'd hit her or something. I could feel my face turning red. I can be such a jerk sometimes. "Look, uh, Case, I didn't mean to yell at you like that. It's just that . . ." My voice trailed off.

"Sure, Shane," she said coolly. She nodded toward the open door. "This is your stop. You'd better get off."

I stood up, fumbling to gather up my book bag, my spare runners, all that junk that comes out of your locker on the last day of school. "Casey, I . . ." I tried again.

"Bye Shane." She turned to look out the window.

Whatever thoughts I had right then disappeared when a strange sound emerged from the front of the bus. It was my buddy Alvin, who, like half the seven year olds in Alberta, had lost his front teeth this year and was having a little trouble with his s's. "For Pete'th thake, Thane, are you gonna thtand there all day? Hurry up and get off tho I can get home. I gotta go to the bathroom."

I couldn't help laughing, but seeing that Alvin was dead serious I thought it best to get moving. "Hang tough, Alvin, I'm outta here." I gave him a grin and tipped his cap over his eyes on my way down the steps.

I was still grinning as I dumped my book bag on the back step and dug the house key out of my pocket. But as I opened the door and the silent emptiness of the kitchen came out to meet me, I felt the grin fade.

This was too much like last summer, I thought; coming home to an empty house, not knowing where Dad was or when he'd be back — or *if* he'd be back. We'd been new here then, new at having the ranch and trying to live settled down like normal people. And Dad had been new at trying to stop drinking.

There had been times — most of the time — that summer when I didn't think we were going to make it. But somehow we had. Somehow we'd managed to forget the past. No, that's not true. There was stuff we could never forget. Stuff we didn't want to forget. Like my mom, who died in a car crash six years ago. But if we didn't forget we did learn to forgive. It took me a long time to forgive Dad for drinking before he drove the three of us into that crash, but I could see that it took him even longer to forgive himself.

Things had been going better since then. Dad had managed to borrow enough money to get started in cattle. Not just ordinary, peaceful old moo-cow cattle. That wasn't Dad's style. He'd got himself a herd of Brahmas. As in Brahma bulls. Rodeo bulls. The kind Dad had spent about ten years of his life riding — and another couple of years playing tag with when he was a rodeo clown. You'd have thought he would have had enough of bulls, but not Dad.

There were three young bulls in the bunch, 1,500-pound honkers, with big humps on their shoulders, the personalities of Mafia hit men, and the brains of the Three Stooges. Dad had really loved them. But there was a rodeo stock contractor in Montana who loved them to the tune of five thousand bucks apiece. So Dad kissed Larry, Moe, and Curly goodbye, and loaded them into the stock trailer — he was getting another thousand for delivering them. That was last Friday and I hadn't seen hide nor hair of any of them since.

I hadn't worried when Dad was a day late. Dad's never punched a clock in his life and he measures time a lot looser than most people. It didn't even surprise me that he hadn't phoned to tell me he'd be a little longer than he'd thought. He doesn't think about responsibility quite the way most people do, either. Now that he was two days late, though, I knew something was wrong, really wrong. But I didn't know what to do about it.

I poured myself a glass of milk and paced around the kitchen trying to think it through. If Dad had been in a car wreck and was in the hospital he'd let me know — unless he was dead. My throat seized up and I almost choked on my milk. I'd already lost one parent in a car crash and I didn't think I could go through it again. But if he was dead someone would inform his next of kin, which was me. So what did it mean that he was just plain missing?

It had crossed my mind about a million times to call the RCMP and get them to ask the Montana cops to check on him. But one thing always stopped me. Dad's history — a lot of which he'd spent with a bottle in his hand. What if he'd met up with some of his old buddies and gone off on a four-day binge? It wouldn't be the first time he'd done something like that, just the first time he'd been this far away when it happened. If I called the cops it could set off a chain reaction like the kind that sets off a nuclear warhead, and I wouldn't be able to stop it before it blew my world apart.

When Mom's father died and left us this ranch

there were strings attached. Strings to tie Dad down to this piece of land. If we wanted the ranch we had to live here and look after it. When the busybodies that run the world find out that Dad has abandoned the place — and his fifteen-year-old kid — to go on a bender in Montana, they might just decide he's not living up to the rules. And they'll probably think he's not being a proper parent. I came real close to landing in a foster home last summer and it sure wasn't a scene I wanted to repeat.

I'd finished my milk and just about paced a hole in the kitchen floor, but I still wasn't any closer to knowing what to do. I had to get outside and breathe some fresh air. Dad had said he wanted to cut the west hayfield as soon as he got back, if it was dry enough. I could go see if the ground had firmed up since the last rain. It would give me a good excuse to ride Angel and put off a decision for another hour.

I found Angel drowsing in the small pasture with the other horses. She was easy enough to catch, but when I tried leading her to the barn she hesitated, none too anxious to go to work on a hot afternoon. Reb, my old horse, who has been known to keep me running around the pasture for half a day trying to catch him, came down with a fit of jealousy and almost climbed into my pocket for some attention. Angel laid back her ears and threatened to kick his teeth in if he didn't get out of her way. Reb got the picture. Mares are generally a little more aggressive than geldings.

I threw the saddle on Angel and climbed on, a little disappointed that she behaved like any other broke horse these days. I kind of missed the little rodeos we used to have when I first started riding her last fall. Today I was lucky to nudge her into a reluctant trot as we headed out to the alfalfa field.

The hay was tall this year. Thick and green, it brushed my stirrups as I rode into it. Any other time, Dad would have had my hide for riding through the hay and tramping it down, but this time it was his idea. After all the rain this spring, he'd been wondering if the ground would be too soft to hold up the tractor when he started haying. So here I was, riding slowly through the tall alfalfa, staring down to see how deep into the mud Angel's hoofs were sinking.

Angel must have figured she'd died and gone to horse heaven. With every step she leaned down and stole a bite of delicious chin-deep hay. Gradually her speed dropped to somewhere between slow and stopped, but I was concentrating too hard on the ground to argue with her. Her hoofs were sinking in all right, but not all that much.

Right then, with Angel half asleep and me leaning down over her shoulder with the reins hanging slack, a black creature came tearing up behind us, sizzling through the tall hay like a bullet.

Suddenly Angel erupted. I don't know what she thought she heard or saw, but I do know that if she was a wild horse she'd live to a ripe old age with those reflexes. Before I could even breathe, she'd gone from half asleep to out of control. I felt her back muscles tense up, then we were sailing through the air — not exactly together.

Somehow I managed to stay on Angel's back, but I wasn't in the saddle. I landed sitting behind it. And if that horse wasn't spooked before, she definitely was now. She lit out across that field running and bucking as though the devil himself had ahold of her tail. Every jump shook me a little farther back on her rump. The only thing keeping me from falling off was the white-knuckled grip I still had on the reins.

Believe it or not, I had time for a short conversation with myself at that point. It went something like, "Well, stupid, you really are in a mess, aren't you? You've got two choices: hang on until you finally slip off the back end and wind up with a hoofprint where your teeth used to be. Or, dredge up the guts to let go while you still can. Which is it gonna be?"

I finally had to let go. There was a very short flight through the air, followed by a very sudden landing on hard ground. That's when the lights went out . . .

Chapter 2

Slowly I dragged myself back to consciousness and tried to remember why I was lying in a field that smelled like hay with the wind knocked out of me. I'd just been riding along when . . . Oh, yeah, now I remembered. Something had spooked the living daylights out of Angel. Something big and black. A bear? A bear that was now going to add injury to insult by having me for lunch!

My face felt funny. Wet. Oh, great. What was bleeding this time? Still too stunned to open my eyes, I reached up a cautious hand to inspect the damage and touched . . . fur. *Fur?!*

My eyes shot wide open and I found myself looking into the most beautiful pair of brown eyes I'd ever seen. They belonged to a dog. A black dog, with the world's worst case of morning breath. She was licking my face and scratching at my shoulder with her front paw. It was anybody's guess whether she was trying to revive or bury me.

I came back to life in a hurry. "Hey, knock it off, dog," I said, sitting up and looking around for Angel, who by now was grazing peacefully a few yards away. At least I didn't have to walk home. I looked back at the dog sitting there watching me with a big doggy grin on her face. Where did she come from anyhow? How did she happen to show up right after the bear spooked Angel? Suddenly, it clicked. I must have hit my head to be this slow to figure it out. This *was* the bear.

"Well, you dirty, lowdown, egg-sucking cousin of a coyote! This was all *your* fault. Haven't you got any more sense than to come rippin' up out of nowhere behind a horse like that? You're lucky you didn't get your head kicked in. *I'm* lucky I didn't get *my* head kicked in. You should be ashamed of yourself, you ugly mutt."

The dog took all that in, cocked her head sideways, thought a while, then lay down and rolled over twice, ending up on her back with all four feet in the air, giving me a big, white-fanged, upside-down grin. I glared back at her. "It ain't funny and you ain't cute." I dragged myself to my feet, relieved to find that although *everything* hurt, nothing hurt bad enough to be busted. My left ankle was throbbing pretty good but that didn't worry me much. Ever since I smashed it in a motorcycle accident last summer it complains real easy.

I limped over and gathered up Angel's reins. As I pulled her nose up out of the clover, she blinked her long white eyelashes and gave me an offended look. I gave her a piece of my mind. "And don't go givin' me that innocent look, horse. Believe me, you were named all wrong. Angel you ain't, baby." I swung into the saddle and turned her toward home.

The dog automatically fell into step beside us, her long black tail wagging like it was a propeller and she was about to become airborne. "Oh no you don't!" I yelled at her. "Get outta here!" The dog grinned and wagged even harder. I nudged Angel into a lope. "Go away!" I yelled over my shoulder. The dog speeded up and passed us with a triumphant look on her face.

That did it. I was riding a quarter horse with a racing pedigree a mile long and no Heinz 57 was going to outrun us. I leaned low on the palomino's neck and touched her with my heels. Instantly she broke into a run, the ground sliding by so smooth it felt like Angel was running on wheels instead of hoofs. The trees along the field were a green blur. I looked back to see how far behind we'd left the dog. But she wasn't there. Right then a movement on the other side of us caught my eye. It was that black dog, running right alongside, almost even with my stirrup. Her ears were flat back in the wind, her tail streaming out behind like a pirate banner, and she was matching Angel stride for stride.

I nudged Angel into overdrive and watched over my shoulder as the dog started to fall behind. That was better. The mutt could run, all right, but she couldn't run as fast as Angel. By the time we turned the last corner and headed for the yard she was nowhere in sight.

Angel slid to a stop in front of the barn and I jumped off. "All right, baby! Nice run," I congratulated her, loosening the cinch so she could get her wind back. She was pretty hot, so I figured I'd better walk her around a little. I led her around behind the barn, through the small pasture, and back out in front.

That's where I saw the dog again. She was lying over by the house, gnawing on something blue.

"What . . ." I dropped Angel's reins and went charging over to see what that miserable mutt had got into. I was just in time to see her finish chewing a hole in my school bag and daintily nose out last week's bologna sandwich. "Now look what you've done!" I yelled. "Put that down!"

Sandwich half in her mouth, she looked up at me, then very slowly spat it out and took a step backwards. Her sad brown eyes never left my face as her long pink tongue licked her chops in hope of a stray crumb.

I picked up the now air-conditioned bag. "Look at that!" I snarled, wiggling a finger through the damp hole in its side. "It's totally wrecked."

The dog whined, rolled over, and played dead. I looked at the skinny mutt with the matted fur. I looked at the holey bag. Then I took a mental look at myself, standing there lecturing a dead dog about a bag full of sweaty socks and rotten bologna, and I started to laugh. The dog cautiously opened one eye. When I didn't snarl at her she opened the other and began a belly-crawling sneak toward the remains of the sandwich. I gave up. "Okay, okay, you can have it."

She didn't eat it. She *vacuumed* it up. There was a sort of a GLUP, and voila! (I did a little better in French than math) the sandwich was gone. The dog grinned and looked around for more. "Don't push your luck," I muttered, and pretended not to notice that she fell into step behind me as I led Angel out to the pasture.

Bored and lonesome, in spite of my new four-legged friend, I wandered around trying to find something to do. That shouldn't have been hard. On any ranch there are always about forty times as many jobs as there is time to do them.

Finally I wandered over to where Dad's old truck — the one with the faded JOSH MORGAN: RODEO CLOWN on the side — was parked. The old Ford was about ready to move on to that big parking lot in the sky, but it still ran, and since it wasn't worth selling, we kept it. I strolled around it and checked the tires. Bald, but round. Even the spare held air — at least as long as it was bolted to the front bumper and not holding up any weight.

I don't know how long I'd been leaning on the fender staring at Dad's name on the door and thinking before I opened it and started digging through the glove compartment. Sure enough, the worn and coffee-stained road map was still there. I took it out and spread it on the seat beside me, Alberta side up. There was big old Highway 2 heading out of Calgary and running straight for the border like an outlaw with the sheriff on his tail. I traced the wide red line south until I ran out of paper and then flipped the map over.

Montana. Wide-open, empty Montana — Big Sky Country they called it, and I could see why. It looked as faraway and lonely as the night sky, the far-apart towns like stars sprinkled across it and tied together by the highways playing dot-to-dot between them. Great Falls, Anaconda, Missoula, Butte — the names ran through my head like the names of the places in that old song about the guy who's been everywhere. Miles City, Choteau, Kalispell, Whitefish — yeah, when it came to Montana, I guess I *had* been everywhere, almost anyway. When Dad was rodeoing we'd been back and forth across the whole state a hundred times. And every town had a memory, most of them of the rodeo grounds and who rode and who won and how Dad had done.

We'd had some good times in Montana — and one time so bad I still couldn't even stand to remember it. I made myself concentrate on the names instead. Helena, Billings, Bozeman — Bozeman, that's where Dad had been headed. I studied the map. It was a long way to Bozeman. Right down to the south end of Montana and almost into Wyoming. I tried to figure out how far it was. Were those little figures on the highways in miles or kilometers? They used miles in the States, didn't they? Dad always talked in miles no matter what the road signs said, and changed them back and forth in his head. You were supposed to multiply by 0.6 — or was that divide? Sounded like math to me. I folded up the map and went into the house.

Inside, I spread out the map again. Then I took out my wallet. I still had forty-six bucks left from my last paycheque from the vet clinic. How far did forty-six bucks take you? Not far enough. Then I remembered the emergency fund Dad kept in his sock drawer. He used it to buy himself a bottle when he got really desperate. Lately there hadn't been any bottles. So was there still an emergency fund?

I went into his room and opened the drawer. Two pairs of socks, both with holes, four extra socks that didn't match, and . . . two twenty-dollar bills! I took the money back to the kitchen. So I had the cash and I had the wheels. But did I have the guts to actually do it?

Chapter 3

All I could decide at that moment was to find something to eat. I'd been up to Casey's place for supper three or four times this week, but the rest of the time I'd done all right on my own. I opened the cupboard door and stared inside for a long time trying to choose between all the different gourmet dishes I knew how to make — Kraft Dinner with White Cheddar, Kraft Dinner with Cheese and Tomatoes, plain Kraft Dinner. I closed my eyes and grabbed a box.

I boiled up the macaroni, stirred in the other gunk, and sat there staring wearily at the revolting mess in the pot. Boiled worms for the fourth time this week. Suddenly I wasn't so hungry after all.

But I sat down and started shoveling it in with one hand while the other traced the route to Bozeman.

All of a sudden something slammed into the back door with the force of a runaway truck. I was so startled I almost choked on my macaroni. It was that rotten dog again. She was standing on her hind legs with her front paws on the door and her nose pressed against the little window at the top like a kid at a candy store. Her eyes were fastened on my supper and she was whining real loud.

"Go away," I growled, "I ain't feedin' you again." She scratched at the door and the whining increased in volume. I looked at her big sad brown eyes and then I looked at the rubbery mass of macaroni glued to the bottom of the pot. "Oh, what the heck . . ."

I set the pot on the floor and opened the door. The dog literally fell into the kitchen, skidded across the floor, and homed in on the macaroni like she had radar. Thirty seconds later the pot was polished cleaner than when I'd started cooking with it. I wondered if anybody would ever find out if I just put it back in the cupboard that way.

The dog sighed contentedly and flopped down under the table with her nose on her paws and went to sleep. I went back to studying the map. How many miles to the liter or kilometers to the gallon or . . . The whole thing was giving me a pounding headache. Then I realized that some of the pounding was coming from outside. Hoofbeats. I looked out just in time to see Casey jump off her horse and tie him to the fence. I opened the door and met her on the porch.

"Hi Case," I said with a grin, trying not to show how relieved I was that she was still speaking to me after what I'd said on the bus.

"Hi Shane. What're you doin'?" Before I could answer, the dog noticed we had company and came barreling out to jump up on Casey and lick her face. Casey laughed. "Well, who are you?" she asked, scratching the dog's ears but looking at me for an answer.

I shrugged, "Your guess is as good as mine. I was out checking the hay when she came tearing up behind Angel and spooked her seven ways to sun-down. Next thing I knew the mystery mutt was lickin' my face and I haven't been able to get rid of her since."

Casey gave me a puzzled look. "How could she lick your face if you were on the horse?"

"I wasn't *on* the horse anymore," I said sourly, glaring at the dog.

Casey burst out laughing. "You got this big-time cowboy dumped off his horse, Miss Tree? What a bad dog!" Miss Tree — or whoever she was — just grinned and wagged proudly. I had a feeling that sympathy was downright scarce in this crowd.

We all went inside. Trust Casey to spot the map right away. "Going somewhere, Shane?" she asked, bending over to look at it.

I laughed. "Not likely. Just lookin'."

She bought that as if I was trying to sell her the Brooklyn Bridge. "You're going after your dad, aren't you?" she said, her eyes on mine. Lying to Casey is real hard when she looks at you like that.

"Maybe," I said, studying an old scar on my hand like I'd just discovered an archaeological treasure. But those eyes pulled mine up to meet them. I walked over to stare out the window, but she followed.

"It won't work," she said. "You don't even have a driver's licence."

"That won't matter if I don't get caught."

"You'd get caught."

"Thanks for the confidence," I said. There was a long silence.

"I'll go with you."

That turned me around. I laughed. "Sure, Case, your mom would be real likely to let you go to Montana with me." Mrs. Sutherland was pretty laid-back, but she wasn't crazy.

"My mom won't be around. She and Dad are heading for New York at six o'clock tomorrow morning."

"You're kiddin'."

"Nope. One of Dad's clients gave him tickets to a couple of Broadway shows and since it's their twentieth anniversary this summer Dad decided he and Mom needed to go and 'rediscover themselves,'" Casey said, rolling her eyes at that part. She and her dad never did communicate too well.

"How long are they gonna be gone?"

"A week."

"Yeah? I didn't think your mom could stay away from her critters that long."

Casey laughed. "She doesn't think so either. She's already complaining."

"So you're gonna be in charge of the place, huh?"

Casey tossed her head like a pony whose bridle was too tight. "I wish! Mom's vet patients are going to the clinic in town, which is fine. But Aunt Sylvia's coming to *baby-sit* me."

"Who's Aunt Sylvia?"

"You don't know her — for which you should be grateful. She's a health nut. She makes tofu hamburgers and sprinkles bran flakes on her ice cream. And last time she was here she tried to teach me to *crochet*." The way that last word came out it sounded as evil as teaching her to peddle cocaine or something.

Before I could think of a safe answer Casey was off on another roll. "You don't know how lucky you are, Shane. *Your* dad figures you can look after yourself while he's gone. And here I am two months older than you" — she would have to get that in — "and my parents don't think I've got sense enough to come in out of the rain. Boys get all the breaks."

She ran out of steam and sat there glaring at me like it was all my fault, while I thought over what she'd said and remembered times I could have used a little more overprotectiveness from my dad. Like the time when I was ten and he left me alone in a hotel room in some Wyoming town while he went out for a drink, or twenty, busted up the bar, and spent the night in jail. But I didn't tell Casey that. It came too close to what I was thinking might have happened to him this time. Instead I asked, "Can't you go to New York with them?"

That brought on another head toss. "Sure. Mom said I'd be welcome to come. But I know they're thinking of this as sort of a second honeymoon, so I can imagine how much they'd enjoy having me tag along. Besides, the show tickets are for two. What am I gonna do, sit in a hotel room watching TV and wait to get mugged?"

That seemed like the sort of question there isn't a real good answer for. I didn't have to answer, though, because right then Casey checked her watch. "I gotta go," she said, heading for the door. "Call me first thing in the morning and we'll go riding or something." Halfway across the room she stopped and gave me a hard stare. "*If* you're still here in the morning."

"Sure I'll be here in the morning," I said, not quite meeting her gaze. It was the truth. I wasn't going anywhere tonight.

Chapter 4

I went to bed early, but for all the sleep I got I might as well have spent the night playing basketball. Oh, I guess I slept some, but I couldn't stop dreaming about Dad. Every time I closed my eyes I'd start seeing him dead on the floor of some far-off McDonald's because he'd made the mistake of stopping for a burger when some guy was about to flip out and start shooting. Or I'd imagine him burned beyond recognition in a truck wreck with the Three Stooges turned into smoking sirloins in the trailer behind him. Or else I'd see him alive and well, but so pickled in alcohol that he couldn't even recognize himself . . .

To tell the truth I'm not sure which scene scared me the most. But I woke up the next morning knowing one thing for sure. I wasn't going through another night of sitting here just wondering. I got dressed, tossed some clean underwear and a spare shirt into my holey school bag, and found a couple of fairly elderly apples for breakfast. I threw the rest of the apples and some cheese and crackers into a bag. There, I was packed.

I was about to head out when there was a now-familiar thud against the door, and I looked up to see Miss Tree eagerly staring in at me again. "Okay, okay, one last breakfast and then you and me hit different trails, pilgrim." Being all out of leftover Kraft Dinner the best I could do for her was a peanut butter sandwich, which she inhaled like everything else.

I pumped the last of the gas from the nearly empty farm fuel tank into the truck and managed to half-fill the tank. It was purple gas, which isn't legal for anything but farm use, but since I was driving without a licence, one more sin probably wouldn't matter much. I locked the house, took one more look at the four bald tires, and climbed into the truck.

Miss Tree had finished her sandwich and sat looking at me with her head cocked, whining softly. "No, you can't come. Go on up to Casey's place. She likes you." Thinking of Casey sent a surge of guilt through me, so before I could think again I turned the key and roared out of there, leaving a spray of gravel behind me. Dad would've yelled at me for that. But then again, if Dad had been here to yell at me I wouldn't be doing this at all.

I was almost to the first corner before I happened to glance in the rearview mirror. Mostly I saw dust, but right in the middle of the dust cloud was a black dot. I told myself it was a flyspeck on the mirror but I eased off on the gas a little. The speck started growing into a dog, a dusty black dog, with her tongue hanging out so far she looked in danger of tripping over it.

The truck rolled to a stop. The dog caught up. "No," I said, "You can't come. What am I gonna do with a dog?" For some reason I'd opened the door instead of the window to make that speech, and before I knew it the dog shot into the truck, scrambled over me, and arranged her warm, smelly body on the seat beside me. She grinned. I groaned. But I shut the door and drove on.

I drove south, sticking to the backroads instead of Highway 2, because this way I'd be less likely to meet some nosey cop who liked to look at drivers' licences. The sun climbed toward the top of the clear blue sky. Miss Tree panted noisily, slobbered on the windshield, and reached over to slop me gratefully, full in the face with her tongue. Between her and the radio blasting at no-adults-in-the-truck level I should have had enough to keep my mind occupied. But my imagination still kept making little side trips into places I didn't want it to go.

I kept wondering where I was going to spend the night. Not in some four-star motel, that was for sure. On the money I had, I'd be lucky to have enough for gas. I'd have to sleep in the truck in some roadside stop. I was used to that. Dad and I had done it dozens of times. But in spite of all Dad's bad points, I'd always felt safe with him. This time I'd be alone, and a lot of bad stuff happened to people along highways at night. They got held up, they got murdered for the ten dollars in their wallet, or they just disappeared. Some vicious killer slipped up behind them and . . .

Just then there was a knock on the camper window behind my left ear. I swear if I'd been ten years older I would've had a heart attack right there in the middle of the road. Instead, I hit the brakes so hard the truck skidded sideways across the road and narrowly missed rolling over into the ditch. Miss Tree gave a terrified yelp — either because of the killer in the camper or the killer behind the wheel — and somewhere in there I managed a glance over my shoulder.

What I saw didn't look much like your average killer. It looked a lot more like a fifteen-year-old blonde named Casey Sutherland.

Miss Tree and I practically fell over each other getting out of the truck and racing around to the back of the camper. As I reached out to open the door it was flung open from inside and I was face-to-face with Casey. She had one hand on the door handle, and to my amazement, the other was holding a bunch of Kleenex over her bloody nose.

Before I could ask if she was okay she lit into me like a nest of irritated wasps. "Geez, Shane, did you have to hit the brakes like that? My head almost went through the window!"

So much for worrying about whether she was all right. She sounded ready to lick her weight in wolverines. And I wasn't feeling real peaceful myself. "Well how did you expect me to react, pounding on the window like that when I didn't even know you were there. Lucky I didn't total the truck. What do you think you're doin' anyhow?"

"Tryin' to get my nose to stop bleeding," she muttered accusingly, sniffing as she glared at me over top of the wad of Kleenex.

"You know that's — " I began, but a loud blast from a horn made both of us jump. A big gas tanker was sitting in front of the truck, which I'd left blocking both lanes.

I felt as if we'd been caught necking instead of fighting in the middle of the road. Casey and I raced around the camper and dove into the cab of the truck. Miss Tree, who'd been watering a dandelion in the ditch, was a split second behind us, and Casey accidentally slammed the door on the end of her tail. It was just the long hairs that got caught, but Miss went into a dog fit and for a couple of seconds the whole cab was one giant howling tornado of black and white fur till Casey finally got the door open.

When *that* was under control I glanced up at the rearview mirror and saw that a school bus had pulled up behind us, loaded with kids who were all laughing and pointing at us. The kids in this county obviously got out for the summer a day later than us, but from the looks on their faces the entertainment we were providing had made the extra day worthwhile.

I slammed the truck into reverse, but it stalled. I was so rattled I'd shifted into fourth gear instead. I tried again, found reverse, and shot backward and almost into the other ditch before I got things under control.

With the happy school bus hot on our tail, we headed south down the narrow road. It seemed like miles before I found a place to turn off and let the bus pass us. Finally, I pulled onto a side road and the bus roared by, with the kids hanging out the window yelling and waving at us.

We'd covered that distance in total silence, Casey and I glaring straight ahead and Miss Tree, still real put out about her tail, shooting us both nasty looks. As the dust settled I turned to face Casey. Her nose had stopped bleeding and she looked back at me defiantly.

"Case," I said again, "what do you think you're doing here?"

"Going with you to find your dad."

"No way. When your parents find out where you are they'll hit the roof."

"They won't find out."

"Sure they won't," I muttered. "You think Aunt Sarah will be too high on health food to notice you're missing?"

"Aunt Sylvia," Casey corrected. "I took care of her. Left a note saying that at the last minute I'd decided to go along to the States after all. Can I help it if she thinks I meant New York instead of Montana?"

I just shook my head in amazement. This was Casey? Honest, straight-shooting Casey, who, as far as I knew, had never told a lie in her life? "You never used to be this sneaky," I said.

"I never had to be," she said.

"Well, you don't have to this time either 'cause now I'm gonna turn around and take you back home."

"Aw, come on, Shane. I've got fifty bucks for gas money."

"No."

"And by the time you take me home and get back this far again you'll have burned up nearly a tank of gas and wasted the whole day."

"You should have thought of that before you pulled your little stowaway trick."

"Geez, Shane, you didn't even make the *dog* go home so I don't see . . ."

"NO!"

"You just don't get it do you, Shane? For a whole year now we've done everything together. I stuck with you when you crashed the bike and your dad took off on you. I was good enough to be your best friend then. But now, all of a sudden, things change. You give me all this stuff about what my parents would say. That's not really what it's all about. It's because I'm a girl. It's okay for a fifteen-year-old boy to take off on some crazy adventure, but oh, no, not me. I'm supposed to stay home, nice and safe and bored out of my mind, eating alfalfa sprouts with Aunt Sylvia. It's just not fair!"

Casey gulped in a deep breath and brushed her hand across her cheek real fast. Not so fast that I didn't see the tears, though. Casey crying? Casey wasn't one of those girls who turned on the tears whenever she wanted to get her own way.

"Look, Case, I'm sorry," I began, feeling like the

world's lowest excuse for a human being. "I — I just can't take you . . ."

Casey wiped her sleeve across her face and then looked me straight in the eye. "Okay, Shane, let's cut to the chase here. I'll sleep in the cab. You sleep in the camper. Does that solve any of your problems?"

I felt my face get real warm and kind of wished I could just disappear. Casey did have a way of covering all the bases without using up too many words. "Aw, Case, I just don't know . . ." I said, starting the truck and wheeling it back in the direction of the main road. I meant it. I *didn't* know. But at the intersection the truck somehow turned itself south, toward Montana.

Chapter 5

Neither of us said much for the next hour or two. I was still half mad at Casey for even being there, and I think she figured that now she'd got what she wanted she'd better lie low for a while and not push her luck. She sat there studying the map of Montana like it held all the secrets of the universe. Maybe it did. If it held just one I'd be satisfied.

At last I broke the silence. "Hope you've got that map figured out. We're about to start usin' it."

Casey glanced up and gave me a questioning look. Then, spotting the group of buildings and flagpoles up ahead she did a double take. "*That's* the border?"

"Sure. Why's that such a surprise? We've been headin' for it for nearly four hours."

She took a fast survey of the area and then pointed at a little side road that led into somebody's cow pasture. "Turn in there, quick!"

"What for?"

"Just do it, Shane!"

I did it and she let out her breath in a relieved sigh. "That was close."

"Huh?"

"What are we gonna do about the dog?"

I looked at Miss Tree. She seemed fine. "What's the matter with her?"

Casey sighed again and shook her head like she'd come up against a real slow person. "They won't let her across the border just like that, you know."

"Why not? She's a Canadian citizen. She doesn't have a criminal record, unless horse-spookin' counts as a serious crime."

Casey explained. "She's gotta have proof her vaccinations are up-to-date and everything. People getting ready to spend the winter in Arizona are always bringing their dogs to Mom for that before they leave."

I looked at Miss Tree sitting there with her usual happy-stupid grin on her face. Then I looked at Casey. She didn't look too worried, either. Obviously neither one of them understood the situation. "Well, it's a little late to bring that up. We sure don't have time to go hunt up a vet. And we're not gonna leave her behind," I added, just in case Casey was getting any ideas.

She just shrugged. "No big deal," she said. "We'll just put her in the camper and cover her up."

I looked at that black-and-white-furred bundle of hyperactive hound. "You gotta be kiddin'. She'd never be quiet long enough to get away with it."

Casey fixed Miss Tree with a steely look. "Oh yes she will. I'll have a talk with her." She got out of the truck, crawled into the camper, and called the dog in with her. The door shut behind them.

A couple of minutes later Casey came out alone. "Okay, pardner," she drawled, "let's head for the border."

I gave her a doubtful look, but being all out of better ideas, I shrugged and climbed into the truck. As I settled myself behind the wheel she brought her hand out from behind her back. "Oh, yeah, I found something for you back there. Put it on." She brought out a battered old stetson hat of Dad's. It looked as though it must have been stepped on by at least one bull, and I'm sure Dad had given it up for dead.

"What for?" I asked.

"It'll make you look more mature," she said with a grin.

"Sure it will," I said gloomily. "Would have grown a moustache, too, if I'd had the time."

Casey giggled. "Yeah, about four years." I gave her a dirty look and started the truck.

Traffic had started to jam up behind the border crossing, and it took us about twenty minutes to edge our way up to the checkpoint. Plenty of time for me to realize just how crazy we were to even dream we might get away with this — two fifteen-year-olds without drivers' licences and one dog without her papers all trying to cross an international boundary in broad daylight? By the time the border guards finished with us they'd probably decide we were here to assassinate the president and lock us up, dog and all, and throw away the key.

That was the last thought that crossed my mind as the car ahead of us rolled away and the person on duty signaled us forward. I yanked my "mature" hat a little lower on my head and drove into the valley of death.

There was a woman guarding the border today. She didn't look too dangerous. More like somebody's grandma, actually. That was both good and bad. Grandmas aren't likely to shoot first and ask questions later, but then again, it's real hard to lie to them. I hoped I wouldn't have to.

"Good afternoon," she said, smiling as she leaned over to look in the window. "Beautiful day, isn't it?"

"Uh, yes ma'am," I said, careful not to make any false statements if I didn't have to.

"And what is the purpose of you folks' visit to the United States?"

"We're on our way to Bozeman to meet my dog, uh, I mean my dad," I stammered, feeling my face start to turn the color of an overripe tomato. I sounded guilty as sin.

The guard studied my face for a few long seconds and I had to fight back a wild desire to pull the hat right down over my eyes. I could tell she was wondering how old I was. I *knew* she was going to ask to see my driver's licence. "And what's your dad doing in Bozeman?" she asked.

I didn't suppose the truth could hurt and I was way too rattled to think of a lie anyhow. "Taking a load of rodeo bulls to a stock contractor there," I said.

She thought that over. "Say, did he go through here about a week ago by any chance?"

I nodded. "Yes, ma'am."

Her gaze shifted and I could see her studying the faded JOSH MORGAN, RODEO CLOWN on the side of the truck. Her eyes came back to me and she said in kind of an amazed voice, "So that really was *the* Josh Morgan?"

"Yes, ma'am," I said, being kind of short on vocabulary right at the moment.

"Josh Morgan," she repeated. "I remember watching him ride bulls ten or fifteen years back.

He was the best. Hasn't been a bull rider like him since he retired. Good lookin' devil, too, with that blond hair and big smile of his." She took a closer look at me — as much as she could see under the hat. "Yeah, there's a resemblance all right," and I turned red for the second time in two minutes. "Well, you say hi to him from one of his biggest fans, you hear?"

"Yes ma'am." A trained parrot could have said something more intelligent, but at least this way I wasn't making any more "dog" comments.

"Okay, we better get on with business here," she said, and my heart sank. "Duration of your stay in the U.S.A.?"

How am I supposed to know? Till I find my dad. A day? The rest of my life? I snatched a figure out of thin air.

"About a week."

"Okay. No fresh fruits and vegetables?"

I shook my head. "No pets, I see," she said, glancing around the cab of the truck.

No, ma'am, I thought, keeping my mouth firmly shut. None that you can see.

"Okay, I better take a glance inside the camper and then you can be on your way."

That did it. We were dead. A picture flashed across my mind. It was from some public service commercial that used to be on TV. These good, red-blooded, upstanding Canadian kids cowering in some foreign jail. That was going to be us. The commercial was about smuggling drugs, not dogs, into the country, and I think the jail was in Turkey or Peru instead of Montana, but it seemed close enough for me. I have an excellent imagination at times like this.

"If you would just open the camper . . ." the guard began as I sat there frozen to the seat. Just then she took a look over her shoulder and gave kind of a pained moan. "Oh, no, they're migrating again."

I stared at her, wondering what she was talking about, then I looked in the rearview mirror and I saw them. It was like the stories I'd read about locusts or army ants on the move. There were dozens of them, all lined up one behind the other, their shiny armor gleaming in the sun. Aluminum trailers — Airstreams, I think they call them — and they were all lined up on the highway behind us, waiting for their turn to cross the border.

The border guard looked like she'd suddenly come down with a megamigraine. "Why me, Lord?" she groaned. "Why do these caravans always come through when *I'm* on duty? They'll have traffic backed up halfway to Calgary." She glanced back at us like she'd almost forgotten we were there. "Go ahead," she said impatiently, motioning with her hand like she was sweeping us right out of there.

I didn't hesitate. In thirty seconds the border had disappeared behind a Montana hill, and I let out the breath I'd been holding for so long I was about to turn blue.

Just then there was a loud bark. I looked around to find Miss Tree's nose flattened against the back window and her paw scratching furiously at the glass. I shot Casey a sideways grin. "That's how you looked back there with your nose pressed against the glass," I said as I pulled over to the side and stopped.

I jumped out fast before Casey could hit me, and let the dog out. Miss Tree almost knocked me over as she covered my face with smelly kisses, then jumped into the truck ahead of me, barking excitedly as we drove back onto the highway. "Case," I said admiringly, "I gotta admit it. You're a genius. How'd you get her to settle down in the back like that?"

Casey gave me a grin that made her dimples show. "Really want to know my secret?"

"Yeah."

"Well, I just fed her a whole dish of leftover lasagna I'd brought along for our lunch."

My stomach, not fed since my puny breakfast seven hours earlier, sat up and gave a howl of pain. "You brought lasagna and fed it to the *dog*?" I moaned.

Casey just laughed. "Hey, it got us into Montana didn't it?"

At that moment we rounded a bend and I saw something that would just about save my life.

Chapter 6

Just off the highway was a little cluster of buildings, a convenience store, a burger joint, and a gas station. Relieved as I was to avoid starvation, I was even more relieved to see the gas station. I hadn't mentioned it to Casey but the needle on the gas gauge had been sitting somewhere on the dangerous side of empty for about the last twenty miles. "Am I glad to see this place," I said, wheeling up to the pumps.

Casey leaned over to check the gauge. "Wow, don't believe in cutting it close or anything, do you?" she said.

I grinned. "Yeah, it was a little tense there for a while but I wanted to get across the border before I bought gas."

"Why?"

"Gas is way cheaper in Montana. Dad always worked it so he filled up on the south side of the border."

"Oh," Casey said, impressed with all my worldly knowledge. "While you get gas why don't I run over and pick us up a burger?"

"Best idea you've had all day. I'll have a double cheeseburger, large fries, a Coke, and — "

"Whoa! Back off, you bottomless pit! We've got to make our money last all the way to Bozeman." She jumped out and I told the gas jockey to fill it up. I checked the price on the pump. Yeah, gas *was* cheap in Montana.

When the tank was full I handed the guy a twenty. He stared at it for a minute. "You don't have any American?"

I gave him a blank look and then clued in. American money was one detail I'd never thought about. "Uh, no. Don't you take Canadian?"

The guy shrugged. "Sure. No problem." He disappeared inside with the money. A minute later he was back. "Need another buck and a half."

"What? At that price it couldn't possibly have taken more than seventeen bucks' worth."

"Sixteen-fifty. Plus thirty percent exchange on the dollar." I sat there with my mouth hanging open for a while. Then I handed him the buck and a half.

A few minutes later Casey landed back in the truck, her hands full of foil-wrapped packages and a big bag of dry dogfood. "What a rip-off! You'll never believe what they had nerve enough to charge me."

"An extra thirty percent," I said tiredly. "Welcome to the real world, Case. Don't you wish you were back home?"

Casey stuck her chin in the air. "Nope," she said with a defiant grin. "At least here I'm eating overpriced burgers instead of fighting the cows for a sprout of alfalfa."

I pulled the truck into the shade and we ate our overpriced burgers. In spite of her bellyful of lasagna, Miss Tree begged until we opened the dogfood for her. She gave it a disdainful sniff and went back to whining till we each gave her a bite of burger.

Casey wanted to drive, and I was ready for a rest, so we hit the road with her behind the wheel and me navigating. I had my nose buried in the map trying to figure out where we turned off to get to Great Falls. Dad had said he was going to stop there and pick up a new pair of boots, so I figured we should go the same way and try to find out if he'd made it that far.

All of a sudden Casey said, "Weird!"

"What's weird?" I said, not looking up.

"This state. I keep seeing these little white

crosses in the ditch every few miles. They look like graves or something. What are they into here anyhow? Drive-through cemeteries?"

At first I didn't know what she was talking about, but I glanced up just in time to catch sight of a small, white roadside cross as we went around a sharp curve. Then I remembered. I'd wondered about those crosses the first time I saw them, too. Mom had explained them to me. Now I told Casey. "Some counties in Montana put up a cross every place that somebody gets killed in a car wreck. Guess it's supposed to make people drive careful or something."

"Oh," Casey said with a shrug — but I noticed her foot lightened up on the gas.

"You know," she said after a while. "We're doing okay. We not only made it across the border, but we found out from the border guard that your dad did come into Montana right on schedule. Things could be a lot worse."

A second later they were. There was a loud bang and the truck skidded to the right. Casey wrestled with the steering wheel and somehow managed to bring the truck to a lurching stop with only one wheel in the ditch. We looked at each other. She was whiter than socks washed in Tide. "What was that?" she asked in a shaky voice.

"Four guesses and all of them are spelled T-I-R-E," I said, jumping out to inspect the damage. Sure enough the right front tire had blown itself clean to kingdom come.

"Wow!" Casey said softly, inspecting the shredded tread lying scattered across the road. And that pretty much summed up the situation.

We spent the next forty-five minutes changing the tire. I'd had plenty of tire-changing practice, so the method was no problem. But those wheel nuts had been tightened by either Superman or an air wrench. It took both me and Casey leaning on the wrench together — plus Miss Tree barking encouragement with all the energy and intelligence of a Dallas Cowboys cheerleader — to get them loose. But finally, hot, tired, and dirty, we were back on the road — with three semibald tires, one very bald tire, and no spare.

I was driving again, taking it easy, maybe a little more shook by the blowout than I wanted to admit. There wasn't much traffic on this road that wound and climbed through the hills. Most of the big-time tourists probably crossed the border farther east on the main highway.

It was real pretty here at this time of year with all the wildflowers blooming and the grass still green from the spring rains. Gradually I felt the tension starting to ease out of me. Here I was, driving down the road with the sun shining, a beautiful girl beside me, and a big, smelly dog perched on the seat between us. What more could I want? To find out if your dad is dead or alive would be nice, a nasty voice inside my head reminded me and spoiled the whole thing.

We passed a big old log building with a sign that read, THE ELKHORN INN. Something about that name stuck in my head but I couldn't remember anything about it. I hadn't been through this part of Montana since I was a little kid. I steered the truck around another sharp curve. Casey pointed off to the left where a small white cross was almost lost in a clump of pink flowers. "Hey look, another roadside graveyard."

I glanced sideways at the spot and, all of a sudden, something clicked in my head. A wall of cold shock slammed into my chest so hard it felt for a second as if my heart had quit beating.

"Shane! Look out!" Casey's words seemed to be coming from somewhere far away. I reacted just in time to jerk the steering wheel around and avoid a big tree at the side of the road. I hit the brake and we squealed to a stop in the shallow ditch. I just sat there staring straight ahead, remembering.

"Shane, what's wrong with you?" Casey was shaking my shoulder. "Shane, talk to me!" But she was still outside the wall. I was in there alone. Just me and the past.

I opened the door and got out, leaving the door

open behind me, and walked slowly up to the top of the ridge, where the white cross stood at the edge of the curve. Yeah, this was the place, all right. It had been dark then. Dark and raining. I remembered the rhythm of the windshield wipers, the country song on the radio, Dad singing along, the secure feeling of being sandwiched between Mom and Dad in the warm truck cab. We'd just passed the Elkhorn Inn. I could see the lights in the windows and the sign above the door.

And I remembered coming around that curve and meeting the headlights of the logging truck. That was the last thing I saw until I woke up in the hospital and found out my mom was dead.

That was six years ago. I'd thought I was over it. I couldn't believe it could still hit me this hard. But now all the memories came flooding back, drowning me. I sat down on a big rock and just stared at the snow-seamed mountains to the west, at the sapphire tip of St. Mary's Lake in the valley below, and at the little white cross surrounded by a sea of wind-rippled wildflowers. This had to be the most beautiful place in the world. Too beautiful a place to die.

I swallowed and tried to blink back the tears Just then I felt a nudge, and there was Miss Tree, whining softly as she laid her chin on my knee and looked up at me with all the sadness of the world in her worried brown eyes. I laid my hand on her head and worked my fingers through the tangles under her ears. "Thanks for understanding, Miss," I said.

"I understand, too, Shane," Casey said softly, coming up behind me with her hand on my shoulder. "It's your mom, isn't it?" I just nodded, not trusting my voice right then.

Please, God, I said silently, wherever she is, take real good care of her.

Just then a single shaft of sunlight spilled through a space in the clouds, touching the cross and making it glow with a light from inside. The colors of the wildflowers brightened and deepened as they rippled in the breeze. It was a trick of the wind, I knew. The sun had been fading in and out like that all afternoon. But still . . .

I stood up and wiped a sleeve across my face. Mom was in good hands but Dad was still my job. I reached out and took Casey's hand. "Come on, Case, let's burn some highway."

Miss Tree was real pleased to have this show on the road again. She galloped ahead to the truck, bounded in through the open door, and took up her ready position, rear end on the seat, paws on the dash, and nose pressed against the windshield. I wondered if Montana had any laws about restraining your dog with a seatbelt.

"I'll drive," Casey announced. "You can baby-sit the mutt."

I squeezed in and did my best to fold the dog into a more convenient traveling shape as Casey eased the truck back onto the narrow road. I didn't look back as we rounded a curve and headed south.

Chapter 7

We drove into Great Falls, crossed the river, and saw the huge American flag waving on the hillside. In one way it reminded me of how far from home we really were, but in another it felt like coming back home, since I'd spent the first fourteen years of my life mainly in the States. It was already after five o'clock and I was about to die of starvation again, but Casey wouldn't even let me think of food until we found the western store. "What's the name of it?" she asked.

"The Last Stand Western Store," I said.

"Weird name."

"Not really," I said, pleased that, for once, I knew something that Casey didn't. "It's probably named for General Custer's last stand. Down south of here at Little Bighorn his cavalry took on a whole bunch of Indians and got totally wiped out."

"Not quite," Casey argued. "One cavalry horse survived with an arrow in him, and the Indian boy who used to own him found him and saved his life. So the horse — his name was Tonka — was the only survivor of Custer's army."

I looked at her in amazement. All this was news to me. "No kiddin'? Did you read all that in a history book or what?"

Casey grinned. "More like 'what.' I saw it in a movie on the Disney Channel. The Indian kid was pretty cute. So was the horse."

So much for history. We went looking for the store. I'd been there a lot of times with Dad so I didn't figure I'd have trouble finding it. I was wrong. After half an hour of driving around Great Falls and almost getting rear-ended when I slowed down to gawk a couple of times, I gave in and let Casey ask directions at a gas station.

We finally got to the store just as they were closing for the day. They let us in — barely — and I asked if Dad had been there last week. The first clerk I talked to drew a total blank, but he called the manager over. When I mentioned Dad's name she remembered him right away.

"Josh Morgan? The bull rider? Sure, he was here. Picked out a real fine-lookin' pair of boots. Left 'em here for us to stretch a little. Said he'd be back in a couple a days to pick 'em up." A little frown furrowed her forehead. "That was almost a week ago and he hasn't been back yet. Hope he hasn't changed his mind." Then she brightened up. "But if you're his son you can pick them up for him."

I shrugged, a lot more interested in why Dad hadn't come back for the boots than in the boots themselves. "Sure, I guess I can."

"Good!" She hurried off to the back room and came back with a big Tony Lama boot box. "Here you go."

"Thanks," I said, taking the box and turning to leave.

"Hold on just a minute there, cowboy," the manager said. "They're not paid for yet. That'll be two hundred and thirty-four dollars, including tax."

Well, I just about dropped my dentures. Two hundred and thirty-four bucks? Lady, I don't remember ever *seeing* two hundred and thirty-four bucks all in one place.

We spent ten tense minutes telling the manager why we couldn't just pay that little ole bill and take that fine lookin' pair of boots off her hands.

Finally, we escaped. "Whoa!" Casey said as we landed in the truck, laughing. "For a minute there I thought she was going to hold us hostage till somebody came up with the cash."

"Yeah," I said, starting the truck, "that was a close call. And all that stress made me *really* hungry."

"Me too. Turn in here."

"Where?" I asked, coming to an almost-stop in the middle of the street.

"Right here."

"This isn't a place to eat," I said, pulling in anyway because the guy behind me was laying on his horn. "It's a grocery store."

"No kiddin', Shane. You didn't know they have food in grocery stores?"

"But there's a McDonald's just up the road."

Casey breathed a big sigh. "Shane, we're three hundred miles from home, we don't know when we might ever get home, and we've got less than a hundred bucks for food, gas, and anything else that turns up. We can't *afford* to eat at McDonald's. Now come on and I'll show you how to save money."

"This must be what it's like to be married to a thrifty housewife," I muttered under my breath. But not far enough; Casey gave me a good whack. *Then* we went grocery shopping.

For six bucks we got a loaf of bread, some salami, two bananas, some milk, and a package of cookies. Maybe there's something to this thrifty housewife business after all.

After we'd finished eating, and Miss Tree had chowed down a bowl of dog crunchies and milk, we hit the road. It was only seven so we could make some miles before dark.

We picked the main road that went down through Helena. There was a back way to Bozeman that might have been a little shorter but I couldn't remember what the roads were like and I didn't figure Dad would have taken any chances of bouncing the bulls any more than necessary.

The country started changing as we drove out of the prairie and into big tree-covered hills. The road wound along the Missouri River, and every once in a while we'd pass some old weathered ranch yard huddled there in the river valley out of the wind. Those places always reminded me of scenes from some Louis L'Amour book, where a bunch of outlaws might come loping into the yard, unsaddle their sweaty horses, and head into the house to divide up the loot. Sometimes I think I was born about a hundred years too late. Nothing exciting ever happens anymore — unless you count my dad disappearing.

That thought brought me back to reality and I concentrated on my driving. We were climbing up toward Wolf Creek Pass now. It wasn't a high pass, like you get in the Rockies, but the road was curvy and all uphill, and on the curves that aimed us west, straight into the setting sun, visibility wasn't the greatest.

It was turning into a real awesome sunset as a big thunderstorm brewed to the west and those huge clouds turned red and purple. We reached the summit of the pass just as the light started to fade. There was a turnoff here so I pulled over and we just sat there in silence for a few minutes, watching the fire in the sky burn out and soften into smoky purple.

"Wow," Casey said softly. "It was worth the trip just to see that." The first faint rumble of thunder rolled across her last words, and Miss Tree shifted restlessly and gave a low whine. The wind was starting to pick up. I figured we were in for a storm, and I didn't really want to meet it head on in the dark on this crooked stretch of road. I cut the engine. Casey gave me a questioning look.

"This is as far as we go till daylight," I said, opening the door. "Come on. You can have the camper. I'll just grab a sleeping bag and bring it back here."

"You don't have to sleep in the truck. I said I would. It was part of the deal."

"Case," I said wearily. "I am being gallant. You know, like the old guys who used to put their coats on mud puddles for the lady to step on. *You* are the lady. You're supposed to say, 'Oh, thank you, Sir,' and accept gracefully."

Casey giggled. "Oh, thank you, Sir," she

squeaked in a high ladylike voice. "And which one of us gets the dog, kind Sir?"

"You shall have her, fair lady, to protect you from the creatures of the night," I said in my gallant voice. In my normal voice I added, "Besides, there's more room for her back there."

"Right, Shane," Casey laughed, no longer sounding ladylike. "But you'll be sorry when the creatures of the night get *you*." She whistled to Miss Tree and the two of them crawled inside the camper.

I dragged out a sleeping bag, shut the door behind them, and then went to make myself comfortable in the cab. That was a joke. There is no such thing as making yourself comfortable for the night on a truck seat. But I did my best. After all those years of traveling the rodeo circuit I'd become pretty adaptable when it came to sleeping places. I stretched out with my head against the passenger door and my feet against the driver's and closed my eyes. I was tired enough to sleep, that was for sure, but after all that driving my brain kept playing videos of highways on the inside of my eyelids. It was kind of neat, like my own private video game.

I drove and I drove and I drove, and I was just on the edge of driving right to sleep when the storm hit. And I mean hit. Alberta can toss together a pretty impressive thunderstorm, but I think Montana might have her beat. The wind, the rain, and the thunder and lightning all came barreling in with one mighty blast. With the rain pounding on the metal roof it was like being trapped inside a drum in a heavy metal band. And the light show was right out of a rock concert, too. The blue-white lightning flashes lit up the whole countryside with a kind of ghostly glow, and the truck shook with every crash of thunder. They say you won't get struck by lightning in a vehicle so I snuggled a little deeper into the sleeping bag, pulled it tight up over my ears, and closed my eyes again.

Just then, the passenger door burst open and I almost landed outside on my head. Before I could untangle myself from the sleeping bag a bundle of wet, smelly fur landed on my chest. "Move over, Shane!" Casey was yelling in my ear. I managed to drag myself out from under the dripping dog and scramble into a sitting position just as Casey flung herself onto the seat beside me. She was every bit as wet as the dog, although not so smelly.

"Aw, Case," I said gently, looking at her all hunched up and shivering there in the corner. "You're shakin'. I'm sorry. I should've realized you'd be scared back there by yourself in all that thunder and lightning."

Another flash lit up her face in time for me to catch a look that could have peeled paint. "Scared?" she sputtered. "I'm not scared, you dope. I'm *wet!*

No wonder you gallantly gave me the camper. It leaks like Swiss cheese. If I'd stayed there any longer I'd have drowned, you — "

A mighty crash of thunder cut off the rest of what she said, which I think was just as well. Miss Tree gave a yelp and flung herself against me so hard I spent the next five minutes picking fur out of my teeth. Maybe Casey wasn't scared, but the dog sure was. Every crash of thunder caused the same reaction.

The storm hung up there for what seemed like hours. It was too noisy to talk. With three bodies — two of them wet — jammed into that small space it got so hot and damp the windows steamed up. Hot stuff, huh? Well, that's how I spent a romantic night parked in the middle of nowhere with a beautiful girl — who was too ticked off to even speak to me — and a dog — a panting, shaking, wet dog, who did aerobics on the seat between us all night.

I was afraid the whole experience might just put me off parking for a lifetime.

Chapter 8

I woke up with a kink in my neck and the dog's tail flung across my nose. Casey woke up still a little damp and still more than a little ticked. I just gave her a grin and handed her the rest of the cookies. "Come on, Case, live it up. No way you'd be gettin' cookies for breakfast from Aunt Sophie."

"Sylvia," Casey corrected. But she took the cookies and I caught a little grin sneaking across her face.

"You gonna forgive me?" I asked, giving her my best pleading puppy-dog look.

She thought it over. "Okay. On one condition. I get to drive this morning."

I opened the door and slid out from behind the wheel. "Your chariot, my lady."

"Thank you, knave." She slid over into the driver's seat.

The next thing I knew she'd started the engine and driven off, leaving me standing there with nothing but a view of half of Montana. She only drove a hundred yards or so before she stopped and waited for me to come panting up and get in. "*Now* you're forgiven," she said, and we drove on down the road laughing our heads off.

The sun was up now and all that was left of last night's storm was a few puddles along the sides of the road. We were coming out of the high country and the road had straightened out into a long, gentle, downhill slope that made the Ford run like it was young again. The radio was blasting and we were both singing along — not exactly in tune, but making up for it with plenty of volume. I glanced at the speedometer. Hey, we were really tearing up the highway.

"Uh, Case," I said, "you're doin' seventy-five miles an hour."

She checked the speedometer. "No kiddin'! I didn't think this truck had it in her."

We both started to laugh again. "You better not get caught," I warned, turning to open the window and let in some cool air. Then I looked in the mirror and saw a big, green car with some kind of lights on top. "Case, slow down!"

"Why? Am I making you nervous?"

"No, but the patrol car behind us sure is."

She glanced in the mirror. "That's not a patrol car. It's a taxi or something. Highway patrol cars are blue. Remember we saw one back before we crossed the river. They can't be all different colors."

All of a sudden the lights on top of the car started to flash red and blue. "Tell it to the officer," I said wearily. "He wants you to pull over."

Casey jerked her foot off the gas like she'd just spotted a rattlesnake hiding under the pedal. "We're dead," she muttered, steering for the shoulder. As we rolled to a stop she brushed back her hair and took a deep breath. "Let me do the talking, Shane," she whispered as she opened the window.

"Sure thing, Case. Hope it goes better than your driving."

She shot me a nasty look, which she instantly replaced with a five hundred watt smile when she turned to face the cop who came strolling up to the window. "I hope I wasn't speeding, officer," she said, so sweet I barely recognized her.

"Hope again, young lady. Seventy-four miles per hour. The radar doesn't lie."

"Seventy-four miles per hour!" Casey echoed. "Wow, that's fast. I get so confused with miles. In Canada it's kilometers, you know."

"So I've heard." The cop didn't sound real

impressed. He leaned in and pointed at the speed-ometer. "See those little numbers underneath the kilometers? Believe it or not, those are miles."

"Oh, *now* I see them," Casey said, wide-eyed and innocent as a newborn colt that just ate its first clover blossom.

The cop just grunted. Give it up, Case, I thought, wondering why I'd ever let her drive anyway. "Let me see your driver's licence, please," the cop said.

Casey shot me a desperate look. "I, uh, might have put it in the glove compartment. Look and see if you can find it, will you, Shane?"

For a second I just stared at her. Yeah, she might have put her driver's licence in there, if she had a driver's licence, which she didn't any more than I did. I figured she might as well just get on with telling the truth so we could get thrown into that foreign jail just like I'd been expecting ever since we smuggled the dog across the border. But before I could say anything I got smacked in the chops with Miss Tree's tail as she launched herself across the seat and started licking the cop's face like she'd just discovered her long-lost best friend.

"Miss!" Casey yelled. "Stop it!"

I managed to reach up and grab the dog by her collar and drag her back where she belonged. Great! Just what we needed to really annoy this guy. No licence and now he'll think we've got a killer

dog going for his throat. "Geez, officer, I'm sorry . . ."
I began, but the cop wasn't listening. He was leaning in through the window, reaching over to rub the
dog's ears.

"Well, hi there fella. Aren't you a beauty? Just
the kind of dog I always wanted when I was a kid.
Bet you're a great cattle dog, huh?"

When the dog didn't answer he glanced in my
direction. Miss Tree gave me a glance, too. Kind of
a snooty one, I thought. Like she was pointing out
to me that, at last, she'd met a human properly able
to appreciate her. Well, that was fine with me. As
long as this guy kept appreciating the dog he wasn't
pushing me to find the licence.

"Uh, yeah, real great," I said. "She can really get
horses moving, too," I added, shifting a little on the
seat to ease the bruise on my backside I'd got
courtesy of this truly wonderful mutt.

I didn't know if the cop was even listening. "Stay
here!" he suddenly ordered, and I wasn't sure if he
was talking to us or the dog. He turned and walked
off toward his car.

"Bet he thinks we stole the truck and he's gonna
call in the licence number and check it out," Casey
said. "Now what are we gonna do?"

I shrugged. "Beats me, Case. You're doin' the
talkin', remember?"

Just before we had time to get in a real fight the

cop was coming back — to my side of the truck this time. He had a grease-stained paper bag in his hand. "Left over from yesterday's lunch," he said, looking real proud of himself as he dug out a well-ripened bologna sandwich and showed it to Miss Tree. I got the door open just in time to keep her from going through the window. She scrambled over top of me leaving studded-tire tracks across my stomach and had that sandwich inhaled in a split second. The cop grinned. "You're welcome to it, pooch. Just don't tell my wife, okay? Find that licence yet, young lady?" he added absent-mindedly as he smoothed the tangles behind Miss Tree's ears.

"Uh, not yet, sir, but we're still looking." Casey gave me a fierce dig in the ribs with her elbow and I started sifting through the glove compartment junk one more time.

This was stupid. Eventually the guy's patience was going to run out and it would be game over. There was no sense prolonging the agony. "Actually, officer — " I began weakly, but he interrupted me.

"Oh, never mind. I'll let it go this time. You Albertans are good neighbors to Montana, and you kids don't look too dangerous. I'd rather spend my time hunting down the real criminals. You know, scum like the dealers and druggies," he added, his eyes starting to smoulder. "Those are the ones I throw the book at. And even then the penalties are nowhere near as tough as they should be. If I had my way . . ." It must have occurred to him that he was making a speech because he stopped himself there. "But," he added, giving Casey a stern look, "you lighten that foot up, young lady."

"Oh, I will, officer," Casey promised, amazing me with her politeness. She started the engine. Miss Tree's nose came up out of the grass where she'd been checking for stray bologna crumbs. She must have thought we were about to go without her because she shot into the truck like she was rocket powered. As she scrambled across me to her reserved spot in the middle, one hind paw caught something under the edge of the seat and sent it rolling across the floor and out the door. It landed on the pavement right in front of the cop's shiny black boots.

I recognized it right away. It was a great big disposable syringe with a needle on the end of it that was long enough and strong enough to penetrate the hide of a Brahma bull. That's what Dad and I had used it for last spring when one of the young bulls got pneumonia. We were in a hurry that day so instead of running the bull into the corral we just drove the truck out into the pasture and Dad roped and tied him to the tailgate. The bull wasn't real impressed with the whole operation, and there's still a dent in the back fender to prove it. We got the penicillin into him, though, and I hadn't seen the syringe since.

I jumped out of the truck and bent down to pick the syringe up — and almost got my hand squashed under the cop's boot. "Don't touch that!" he ordered with a real stern expression that made him look just like Smoky the Bear when he catches somebody dropping a match in the forest.

"Huh?" was the most intelligent thing I could think of to say.

"Just step back and don't make any sudden moves," he said, never taking his eyes off me as he unsnapped his holster and laid one hand over the butt of his revolver. With the other he reached down, and very carefully so as not to mess up any fingerprints, he picked up the syringe by the very end. He studied it close up like it was about to bite. Then he looked at us and shook his head, regretfully. "Just kids," he said. "That's what they told us at the academy, time and again. You'd have thought I'd have got it through my head by now. They may look like the kids next door but they're still just as guilty. Kids and drugs. It's a plague that's destroying this country."

It finally occurred to me what this guy's problem was. "You mean — you think — " I began and then burst out laughing. "You think that syringe . . ." I made the mistake of pointing at it kind of suddenly. Next thing I knew I was staring down the barrel of his revolver. I stopped laughing.

"I *said*, 'Don't move,'" he said. I stopped moving. Next thing I knew I was up against the truck and being searched for weapons, just like in the movies. He did a real half-hearted job of searching Casey, too, as if his cop instincts were losing out to his gentlemanly instincts. Then he loaded us into the back of the patrol car, again, just like in the movies, right down to the little routine where they make sure you don't bump your head. It was kind of funny, but by then I'd given up laughing.

When he finally got on the road for town I thought he might be occupied with driving enough to dare to open my mouth again. "That syringe was for giving a shot of antibiotics to a *bull*," I said.

"Sure it was, kid. Save the bull for the judge."

Chapter 9

We headed for town, us no-good druggies in the back and Miss Tree riding shotgun for Dirty Harry in the front. We came up behind a big semi driving real slow, and after a couple of miles the cop ran out of patience and switched on the siren so he could get by. Instantly, Miss Tree threw back her head and howled along. You should have seen the look on that truck driver's face when a cop car with a singing dog went ripping past him.

Five minutes of uninterrupted howling later we pulled up outside this little old sheriff's office in a little old cow town that looked like it had been there when General Custer's only surviving horse was a colt. We were unloaded with considerable caution and escorted inside. Another cop, a lot older and a whole lot less spit-and-polished — he was wearing scuffed-up riding boots instead of shiny police boots — was sitting at a desk drinking coffee and reading *The Western Horseman*. He looked up, took off his glasses, and studied us for a minute or two. "What ya got here, Willmore?" he drawled at last, none too excited.

"Narcotics, Mr. Saunders. Possession for sure. Possible trafficking. Maybe even international trafficking. They're from Alberta."

Saunders gave us another narrow-eyed once-over. "What kind of narcotics?"

"Don't know yet. We'll have to send this in to the city and get it analyzed." Dirty Harry held up the syringe, now neatly sealed in a plastic bag.

The old guy's eyes got narrower yet. "Let me see that thing," he ordered.

Harry handed it over. Saunders peered at it through the plastic. Then he opened up the bag, took the syringe out, and took a closer look. Dirty Harry gave a gulp. "Careful, sir, the prints . . ."

Saunders ignored him like a coffee stain on the carpet and fixed a steady blue gaze on me. "Penicillin?"

It was the most intelligent word I'd heard in the past hour. "Yes, sir!" I practically chirped with relief.

Saunders eyed the syringe again and raised his eyebrows. "Must of been a big old critter."

"Eighteen hundred pounds of Brahma bull," I said, so relieved I would have kissed that bull if he'd been handy.

Saunders nodded thoughtfully. "Hoof rot?" he asked.

I shook my head. "Pneumonia."

Saunders nodded again. About that time I glanced in Willmore's direction. He looked as confused as a geologist at a rock concert. "But . . ." he began.

Saunders just shook his head. "Why did I have to inherit a city boy that don't know grass is for cows to eat, not smoke, and that not everything in a hypodermic syringe was designed for taking trips without ever leaving the farm?" He walked over to Willmore and held out the syringe. "Take a close look at that."

Willmore took it gingerly like he was still trying to preserve the prints. "What color is that bit of residue left in the bottom, Willmore?"

Willmore furrowed up his forehead and stared. "Pink?" he said weakly.

Saunders nodded. "Well, the good news is you're not color blind. Yeah, it's *pink*. And it also happens to be penicillin. Just plain old penicillin for cattle. And what you have just done is drag two innocent Alberta tourists in here for the felonious crime of pumping a shot of it into the backside of a sick bull and forgetting to get rid of the evidence. And what I am about to do is take these two dangerous perpetrators down to the Sizzlin' Sirloin and buy them the best steak Montana has to offer in hopes the whole dang continent don't have an international incident over this. You stay here and mind the store," he said with a fierce faded-blue glare in Willmore's direction. He turned back to Casey and me and half the glare disappeared in a wink. "Come on, you two. Let's go preserve the peace of North America."

The steaks were big and juicy enough to preserve the peace of the world — if the world had any peace to preserve — and Miss Tree rated those T-bones even higher than well-aged bologna.

An hour and a half later we were back on the road again, stuffed to the eyeballs and shaking our heads about the kind of luck that turned driving without a licence into drug-dealing and then into steak-on-the-sheriff.

The luck stayed with us until a few miles outside Helena. That's when the highway went all to potholes — or at least that's what I thought at first. I was driving again and Casey was reading the map, trying to figure out how much farther it was to Bozeman. She glanced up and gave me an irritated look. "Do you have to hit every bump in the road, Shane? I can't read the map when the numbers keep jumping up and down."

"I can't help it," I said automatically. "This road is rough." I'd barely got the words out when I realized it wasn't true. The highway wasn't any bumpier than it had been a couple of minutes ago. "Uh-oh," I said, steering to the shoulder.

"What?" said Casey.

I didn't answer. I just stopped the truck and jumped out. Yup, the right front tire was flatter than a road-killed gopher. Next thing I knew Casey was standing beside me. "Great," she said tiredly. "And we don't even have a spare."

"No kiddin'," I said, studying the tattered remains of the tire. "That *was* the spare."

So there we stood looking at the sign that said "Helena 4 miles." Four miles is a whole lot farther when you're walking than when you're driving.

We decided to drive. From the looks of that tire there wasn't much point in worrying about whether driving on it flat would wreck it. It was dead anyway. It might as well be a little deader. So we limped into town doing about ten miles an hour while every driver that passed us honked and waved and made desperate signs to let us know we had a flat tire. We just waved back like fools and kept driving until we hit the first service station.

The mechanic gave us a little lecture about driving on the rim. Then he looked in his book and told us a new tire would set us back seventy bucks —

American, of course. I asked him what a semi-retired tire would cost. He poked around in a dusty pile of junk and finally came up with one that was at least as bald as the other three on the truck. "Forty bucks," he said, grinning through his tobacco-stained teeth.

I laughed. "Try again," I said.

He pointed to the road. "My way or the highway," he said.

Chapter 10

An hour later we were back on the road, one bald tire richer and over fifty bucks poorer. We'd better find Dad in Bozeman. We weren't going to have the money — or the tires — to go much farther. All three of us were hot and tired. Miss Tree was smelling even more like a dog than usual, and Casey was giving me static.

"But your dad must have at least told you the last name of the guy who was buying the bulls."

I shrugged and tried to explain for about the third time. "Casey, I don't *remember* his last name. I don't think I ever even *heard* his last name. Dad always just called him Randy when he talked to him on the phone. He just said he was going to deliver the bulls to Randy in Bozeman."

Casey shook her head. "I just can't believe your dad would take off to Montana and not even leave you the name and phone number of the guy he was going to see. I mean, what if you'd had some kind of emergency while he was gone? How'd he expect you to get in touch with him?"

I slammed my hand against the steering wheel. "Case, give me a break! My dad doesn't do things the way your dad does. Your dad's a lawyer. He has to get the price of a pizza in writing before he can order it over the phone. My dad doesn't operate that way. He doesn't write anything down. He doesn't plan ahead for every possible emergency. He just lives from day to day because that's the only way he knows how. And I'm probably gonna turn out just like him, so if the idea bothers you so much you better quit hangin' around with me."

There was a huge silence, broken only by the sound of Miss Tree whining now and then as she panted damply against the dashboard. The flash of anger burned out of me, leaving the ashes to settle heavily into the pit of my stomach. I risked a cautious glance in Casey's direction. She was staring straight ahead. "Casey, I . . ." I began, but she cut me off.

"Stop the truck, Shane."

Oh great, now I'd done it. "Aw come on, Case . . ."

"I said stop the truck." I pulled over and stopped. She opened the door.

"Casey, please, don't take off. I didn't mean to yell at you like that."

"You finished?" Casey asked coolly.

"Yeah, I'm finished but — " She opened the door a little wider and Miss Tree shot out and disappeared into the ditch. Casey got out, too. "Casey, please don't — "

"Don't what?"

I shrugged. "I don't know. Whatever you were gonna do. Take off walking or something."

Casey rolled her eyes. "Shane, how stupid do you think I am? I'm not about to get out and start walking, here, in the middle of nowhere. I told you to stop the truck because Miss Tree wanted out in the worst kind of way. Didn't you hear her whining?" Right then Miss Tree came bounding back from watering the plants, wagging her tail and grinning from ear to ear. She jumped into the truck and gave an impatient bark to get us moving.

Man, was I brilliant. I gave Casey a sheepish glance. "I thought you were mad at me," I said.

Casey grinned. "I am — kind of. We're never going to find your dad if we have to fight about all the details. And if you're going to throw a tantrum and drive at the same time we'll end up smeared like bugs on the grille of a passing semi. Anyhow, it's my turn to drive."

I gave her a cautious look. "You gonna get picked up for speedin' again?"

Casey just smiled. "Trust me," she said.

What could I say? When we climbed back into the truck she was behind the wheel.

A couple of hours later we rolled into Bozeman. It was a nice, peaceful-looking little city that sat just off the corner of Yellowstone Park. It sure didn't look like a place where anything real bad could happen to someone. I sure hoped that this was one time when looks weren't deceiving.

We drove around town for half an hour just looking things over. I don't know what we expected to find. Dad parked on main street just waiting for us to show up so we could all go home together? Randy, the stock contractor, with his business set up under a big sign in the middle of town? We didn't find either one.

"Pull in here," I told Casey as we came up to a big service station at the end of the street.

Casey shot me a puzzled look. "Why? We don't need gas."

"No but maybe Dad did. Let's see if anybody remembers him." They didn't. Neither did any-body in the other four stations we tried.

"This isn't working, Shane," Casey said as we pulled out into the street again. "He could have been here on somebody else's shift or he might not have got gas in Bozeman at all or maybe this guy *did* see him but just wasn't paying attention. The odds of actually finding someone who remembers him are worse than winning big in Vegas."

"You got any better ideas?"

Casey was quiet for a couple of seconds. "Yeah!" she said, doing a U'y in the middle of the street that probably took ten years off my life. Next thing I knew she'd driven back into the service station lot and parked beside the phone booth. I stared at her. "Come on!" she said, jumping out. "All we have to do is go through the phone book and check all the Randys."

Yup, that was all we had to do, all right. Bozeman wasn't all that big, but two hours later we were only up to the L's. We'd found two Randys and called them both. One was a janitor. The other rang busy the first three times we tried. The next time we got a recording. It said that Randy was all booked up for massages this week but to leave our name if we wanted an appointment next week. Something told me that probably wasn't the rodeo-stock Randy.

We were also writing down the names and numbers of all the people whose first initial was R. We had thirty-seven so far. I let the book fall shut. "And you thought asking at gas stations was a long shot. Do you know how many quarters it would take to check out even the names we have so far?"

Casey nodded. "Yeah," she said tiredly. "A lot more than we've got to spare. So let's try Plan C."

"You mean we have a Plan C?" I asked.

"Sure," Casey said. "Since we're right by the phone anyhow, call home. Maybe your dad's there by now."

I shrugged. "Can't hurt," I said, not too hopefully. I started to dig out some change, but Casey stopped me.

"Call collect," she said.

"Right," I said. I waited as the phone rang. And rang, and rang... It was the most depressing sound I'd ever heard.

At last I hung up and sank down on the ground in the shade of the gas station wall. Casey sat down beside me, and Miss Tree flopped down, laid her nose on my knee, and stared sadly into my eyes. I stroked her head. "Yeah, Miss Tree, so much for Plan C." I turned to look at Casey. "It's no use, Case. I don't know why I ever thought I could just drive down here and find him. We don't have any idea where to even start lookin' and we've just barely got enough money to buy gas to get home. We'll head back in the morning. I'm sorry I ever dragged you into this."

Casey reached her hand over toward my face and I jumped like a head-shy horse. I wondered what I'd done to make her mad enough to hit me. She didn't hit me. She just laid her hand on my forehead for a second. "Nope. You don't have a fever," she said.

"Huh?" I said.

"Just thought you must be hallucinating."

"What?" My vocabulary seemed to have shrunk to one-syllable questions.

"Well, if you think you dragged me into this you must be losin' it. Seemed to me that when you found me in the camper all you wanted to do was hog-tie me and drag me back home."

Yesterday morning? Was it really just yesterday morning when we were back home in Deer Valley, Alberta? It seemed like we'd been on the road for at least a week. I gave Casey a sideways look. "Yeah? Well I should've gone ahead and done it. I hate to think what's gonna happen when your parents find out."

Casey shrugged. "I'll get grounded till my twenty-first birthday — for a start. But it would've been worth it if we could've found your dad. You really want to give up?"

"No," I said slowly. "I don't want to give up. I just don't know what else to do. It's like lookin' for a needle in a haystack."

Casey didn't answer and we just sat there watching the traffic go by for a while. Then, right out of the blue, she asked, "How far is it to Yellowstone?"

I turned to stare at her. She was gazing dreamily off across the hills to the south. "I don't know," I said. "Hundred miles maybe. Why?"

She answered the question with a question. "You ever been there?"

"Yeah, we drove through a couple of times."

"What's it like?"

"A big parking lot."

It was Casey's turn to stare at me. "What?"

"Wall-to-wall tourists," I explained.

"Yeah, but outside of the tourists, what's it like? Did you see Old Faithful?"

"Yeah, we got out of the truck, walked across the parking lot, and got ready to wait twenty minutes or whatever it takes between eruptions, but I guess he saw us coming because the minute we got there he blew sky-high. It was pretty neat."

"I'd sure like to see Yellowstone," Casey said.

I eyed her cautiously. "We're not here on vacation, Case."

She ignored that statement and dragged a brochure out of her pocket. "I picked this up at the last gas station we stopped at. There's a picture of someplace called Mammoth Hot Springs. It's really an awesome looking place. All these colored rock formations built up over centuries from the minerals in the hot springs. It looks like something they would've built in Disneyland except that it's real.

See?" She held the brochure out for me to look at and waited for me to say something. I didn't say anything. She tried again. "Look how close it is, Shane. It's right in the very closest corner of the Park." She looked up at the sky. "There's at least three hours of daylight left. If we start right now we could go see it and almost be back here before dark."

"Casey, if we burn up all that gas sightseein' we probably won't have enough to get home," I said.

"So, if we run short we'll cut lawns or something to get enough money to go home."

"No," I said.

"Please?" she said.

Chapter 11

Ten minutes later we were on the road — and headed for Yellowstone. I was driving and had the radio turned up loud so I wouldn't have to talk, because I was still kind of mad at Casey. My whole world is screwed up and she has to go sightseeing. . . .

A half-hour passed as the miles ticked off and the country passed in a green blur. We were getting close to Livingston where the turnoff was to go south to Yellowstone. I was driving on auto-pilot, going through the motions of steering and watching the traffic while my mind wandered through the dark canyons of the future. What should I do next? Break down and report Dad missing? Here? Go back home and report it to the RCMP? Wait for Casey's parents to get home and tell them the whole story — and hope I survived when they found out I'd taken Casey on a wild-goose chase to Montana? And the one question that wouldn't go away: What *had* happened to Dad?

My imagination was doing one more all-too-realistic production of *Shallow Grave in the Desert* when Casey said something I didn't quite hear the first time. I definitely heard it the second time, though, because she yelled, "Stop the truck!" so loud that I instantly hit the brakes and laid a nice patch of rubber on the highway. It's a good thing nobody was behind us.

I turned to look at her. "Casey, for — " I started angrily, but she pointed at a field across the road.

"Recognize anybody?" she asked.

I looked where she pointed and there they were. Out there grazing with some other cattle like they'd lived here all their lives. Larry, Curly, and Moe. Trust a country vet's daughter to spot them out of nowhere. I just sat there staring at them for so long that Casey finally broke the silence. "Guess this means I don't get to Yellowstone, huh?" she said, straight-faced. Then we looked at each other and started laughing like we'd lost our minds.

A minute later, still giggling, she pointed farther down the road. "Look, there's a gate down there with a sign on it." We drove on down to check it out.

The sign, over a big fancy gate, read, B.J. RANDEE RODEO STOCK CONTRACTOR.

"Randee?" we both burst out at the same time and went into another laughing fit that lasted so long that Miss Tree had to reach a paw over and scratch worriedly at my arm to bring me back to sanity.

More or less under control, we drove on up the long lane to have a chat with good old Mr. Randee.

Before we were even out of the truck the door of the log ranch house opened and a big, tall guy in a cowboy shirt came out. For a minute he just stood there studying the sign on the side of the truck. Then, "Well, whad'ya know?" he boomed. "More Morgans!" He strode up to the truck and stuck out his hand. "I'm Billy Joe Randee, and if you're lookin' for rodeo stock you've come to the right place."

I shook his hand. "Yes sir," I said, wondering if he could hear the relief in my voice. "I think we've come to the right place, all right. But it's Josh Morgan we're lookin' for. He's my dad."

Randee studied me for a while. "Yeah, you're the dead spit of him, all right. Would've recognized you as his son anywhere. And is this your sister?" he asked, turning to shake hands with Casey.

For some reason the question made me go red as a beet. "Uh, no. This is a friend of mine, Casey Sutherland. My name's Shane."

"Good to meet you, Casey and Shane. So now what's this about lookin' for Josh? You misplace him somewhere?"

I sighed. "Well," I said, "it's a long story."

"In that case, come on in the house. We were just about to sit down to supper. You can tell us while we all eat."

"Oh, no, we can't — " I began, but it was no use. Just then the door opened and a tall, redheaded woman came out.

"Jess, this is Josh Morgan's son and his friend. We got enough beans for a couple more? Kids, this is my wife, Jess."

We all shook hands some more, got told about three times that neither Billy Joe nor Jess would hear of us not stopping to eat with them, and landed at a big kitchen table with them, their son Cal, and their daughter Bonnie. I took an instant dislike to Cal — mainly because he was eighteen, tall and handsome, and was charming as all get-out to Casey. Bonnie, who was eight and all missing teeth and freckles, kept staring at me like I was the most wonderful thing that had ever fallen out of the sky and landed in her kitchen.

There were plenty of beans — not to mention potato salad, hamburgers, and apple pie. Billy Joe made sure we'd had two helpings of everything before he was ready to discuss Dad. At last he pushed back his chair, took a swallow of coffee, and said, "Now what's this about your dad?"

That was the question I'd driven across Montana to ask. And now I wasn't even sure where to begin. I thought it over till the silence got long and then I decided to just lay it on the line — more or less. I told him about how Dad had planned to be home three days ago and how I hadn't heard from him since he left. "And," I added, "I don't think he's been in an accident or anything like that, because somebody would have let me know by now. I thought about callin' the cops and reporting him missing but, you know, maybe he's all right and — uh — well, maybe something just came up," I finished lamely. "So I decided I'd come down and see if I could find him myself. We did, that is, Casey and me."

Billy Joe studied my face for a while and I wondered if maybe he knew enough about Dad's past to understand about the sort of things that could have come up. The fact that Josh Morgan was a drunk hadn't exactly been a secret around the rodeo circuit.

"Yeah," he said slowly, "a lot of things can happen to hold a guy up. Actually, I guess I'm one of those things."

"You are?"

Billy Joe nodded. "I talked your dad into staying over an extra night. Guy down east of Billings was tryin' to sell me a couple of bulls and I wanted to get Josh to take a look at 'em for me. He's about the best judge of buckin' bulls of anybody I know.

"Then, when we got home, the neighbor phoned to tell us our fence was down and we had cattle scattered over half the countryside. So Josh decided to stay another day and help with the roundup."

I nodded. Two extra days. Okay, the trail was getting warmer. But that still didn't explain where Dad was now. One thing was for sure, yesterday afternoon he still hadn't got as far as picking up his boots in Great Falls. Unless he was having such a good time he'd forgotten all about the boots. "Did he say anything about which way he was goin' home from here?" I asked.

"Yeah, he was headed for Butte. When we stopped in Billings he saw a poster for the Butte Rodeo that was gonna start the next day. Josh said that since it really wasn't out of his way he might as well stop by and say hello to a few of his old buddies he used to ride with."

I could feel a lump start to settle in my stomach. Getting together with his old buddies was the last thing Dad needed to do. I remembered back last summer when Dad had been off the booze for weeks — until a pair of old friends stopped in. Next thing I knew they'd killed a couple bottles of whiskey and Dad was right back where he started from. "But he wasn't plannin' on hangin' around there," Billy Joe went on. "He said his son was expectin' him home and that you and him had a lot of work to catch up on at your ranch. He was real proud of that ranch. He was pretty proud of his son, too," he added, embarrassing me so bad I had to study the pie crumbs on my plate for a while before I could meet Billy Joe's eyes again. "Yeah, he talked about you a lot. Said he'd been through some tough times last year and if it hadn't been for you he didn't think he'd have made it through."

Dad had actually said that? It left me not knowing what I was supposed to say next. So I decided "goodbye" was as good as anything. I stood up. "Well, uh, it looks like we'd better head on over to Butte, then. Thanks a lot for supper, Mrs. Randee."

She laughed. "Just Jess," she said. "It was my pleasure."

"And thanks for the information," I said to Billy Joe.

He stood up, too. "No problem. And don't worry about your dad. He'll turn up. Josh Morgan is one guy who can take care of himself. But here's my card. If you run into any problems at all here in Montana, just give me a call and I'll come runnin'."

"Thanks," I said, taking the card. We were still

just about broke, and a long way from home, but it sure did help to know we had friends in this country.

"Bye, everybody. Thanks for supper," Casey said.

"See you around, Casey," said Cal. I started to give him a dirty look, but then I remembered my manners and didn't look at him at all.

"Bye, Thane," Bonnie said with a toothless grin. If she ever came to Alberta I would have to introduce her to my friend Alvin.

So we hit the road again, knowing for sure now where we were going. We just didn't know what we'd find when we got there.

Chapter 12

It was dark by the time we got back to Bozeman. "Do you want to stay here till morning?" I asked Casey.

She shook her head. "No way. Not when we know for sure your dad was going to Butte. Maybe he's still there and planning to start for home first thing in the morning. Maybe we'll find him yet tonight."

"Maybe," I agreed, but somehow I didn't think it was going to work out that way.

We pulled into a gas station on the edge of town and reluctantly traded a few more of our thin supply of dollars for a full tank. Miss Tree whined until we let her out of the truck, even though it had started to rain. She trotted off behind some old barrels at the back end of the lot while we went in to pay for the gas.

On our way out, Casey nodded toward the pay phone by the door. "Try calling home again," she said.

I shook my head. "It's no use, Case. Dad's not gonna be there."

"Well, you've got nothing to lose by trying."

"*You* try, then," I said.

"Okay, I will." Casey picked up the phone and punched in the numbers. She stood listening to the phone ringing and nobody answering for what seemed like hours. Finally she sighed and hung up, and I didn't even say I told you so.

When we came out again the dog wasn't back so I whistled for her. She still didn't come. But from deep in the shadows behind the barrels came a menacing growl. "Listen!" Casey whispered, grabbing my shoulder. "Is that Miss Tree?"

"I don't know," I said, reaching under the truck seat to pull out the tire iron, "but if it is she's found something downright dangerous back there. And if it *isn't* her growling, then I'm not sure I want to meet whatever is. You stay here while I go see what's goin' on."

"Dream on," said Casey, falling into step beside me.

We came around the side of a barrel and there

was the dog, her ears cocked forward and the fur on her neck standing up as she stared intently into a tangle of tall grass and old tires. "Come back here, Miss Tree!" I ordered firmly. There was a rustling in the grass and Miss Tree took a cautious step forward instead. She stuck her nose into the shadowy pile of tires to investigate the rustling noise. All of a sudden there was an explosive hissing sound. Miss gave a yelp like she was being murdered and recoiled out of there so suddenly she hit me in the knees and knocked me flat on the ground.

It all happened so fast that at first I wasn't even sure what had hit me. All I could think of was "snake!" There'd been a rattler coiled up in there, Miss Tree had stuck her nose in and he'd bitten her and . . .

I scrambled to my feet and raised the tire iron. "Stay back, Case! I'll get him!"

But I was too late. Casey was already reaching into the maze of tires and scooping something up with her bare hands. "Relax, Shane," she said, laughing. "He's not too dangerous." She was holding a half-grown, dark brown, tabby-striped kitten that was fluffed up to about twice its normal size and flashing green fire from eyes as big as flying saucers. It was still hissing furiously at poor Miss Tree, who was looking about as hangdog as a dog can look, while sadly running her long pink tongue over a bleeding scratch on her black rubber nose.

"Aw, look at him, Shane," Casey said. "Isn't he a little beauty?"

I looked at him. He was wet, his fur was matted with mud, and he looked as though he hadn't had a square meal for a month. "Not exactly," I said.

Casey shot me a dirty look. "Well, he can't help it if he's a little bedraggled. He's had a rough life. But look at those eyes! He's got pride. He may be living like an alley cat, but he's a prince inside. Aren't you, Prince?"

And right then, cuddled safe and warm against Casey's jacket, The Prince agreed. He began to rumble softly. Casey grinned and scratched him behind the ears. "Come on, Shane. We have to find a store that's open."

"What for?" I asked blankly.

"To get some milk for The Prince," she said impatiently, as if anybody but a real slow learner would have known.

"But . . ."

Even in the dim light I caught the warning flash of Casey's eyes. "Did you think I was just going to leave him here to starve?"

It wasn't the sort of question you could answer "yes" to. Besides, the poor little guy *did* look awful hungry. "Okay, okay," I said wearily, "we'll get him somethin' to eat. But that's all. We can't go draggin' a cat all over Montana with us."

"Shane," said Casey in a voice so sweet I knew it was dangerous, "let me explain the facts of life to you. I have spent the past two days of hot weather in the cab of an unair-conditioned truck with a dog who doesn't know the meaning of the word 'bath.' I have taken turns getting slapped in the face with her tail and knocked out by her breath. I have not complained. Now I have news for you. The cat comes along."

"Oh," I said.

A few minutes later we were headed west for Butte. Casey was driving, with The Prince riding shotgun on her shoulder. Miss Tree and I were sulking on the passenger side.

After a while I got too tired to sulk. Too tired to even think, but too wired to sleep, I sat staring out at the empty darkness sliding past the window. Not many farms along here. A few big ranches, maybe. Once in a while a single light stood out like a beacon along a distant range of hills. But mostly there was just the darkness. It reminded me of all those miles of night driving on the rodeo circuit with Dad after Mom was gone. The loneliness of night on the highway, of passing lit-up houses and thinking of the families sitting inside those safe circles of light. Families who belonged somewhere. I used to want to belong somewhere real bad. Well, now I had a place where I belonged. I was just real short on family to belong there with.

There wasn't much traffic at this time of night. Just a few semis, long-distance rigs barreling down the highway like spaceships rocketing through space, looking for a friendly planet. We passed a roadside turnoff. One of those places where truck drivers sometimes pull in for a few hours' sleep. No rigs there tonight. It was deserted . . .

"Stop, Case!" I yelled. Casey jumped like I'd hit her with a cattle prod and landed on the brakes so hard the truck skidded across the road. Those nearly bald tires lost a little more tread while scrawling their signature on the pavement. The Prince dug in his claws and hung on for all he was worth as Casey wrestled the truck to a stop and gave me a glare so fierce I could see it in the near-dark of the truck cab.

"I swear, Shane, if you ever do that to me again I'll . . ."

I ignored her and checked the outside mirror. No traffic. "Back up," I said. "To the turnoff."

"What for?"

"Just do it." She did it. "Turn in," I ordered. And as she did, the lights swept across what I thought I'd seen. Way back in the corner of the turnoff, behind a picnic table and shadowed by the overhanging branches of a big cottonwood tree, was . . .

"Your dad's truck," Casey said.

I nodded. "Yeah," I said, wondering how my mouth suddenly got so dry. "The truck and the stock trailer." She pulled up beside it and then for a few long seconds we both just sat there. A lot of stuff ran through my mind in those seconds. Stuff about all the tourists that had been murdered along American highways in the last few years. I remembered all the news stories about Michael Jordan's dad going missing on a trip somewhere — missing until they found his body, murdered by a couple of teenage kids. At a roadside stop, wasn't it? All of a sudden I felt like I'd landed right in the middle of one of those reenactments on *Unsolved Mysteries* or one of those TV shows that takes you back to the scene of the crime. I was going to open that truck door and . . . I wished I was back in Alberta.

Casey and I looked at each other, and even in the dim glow of the dashboard light I could read her eyes. She was thinking the same thing I was. She reached out and put her hand on my arm. "I'll look, Shane." I shook my head.

From the first day I met her — when I was busy getting beat up by the school tough guy until she ran him off — Casey had never known the rules. That *guys* are supposed to do the hard stuff.

Without exchanging another word we both opened our doors. Casey carefully kept The Prince inside but Miss Tree bounded excitedly out and started checking all the trees and posts for messages from previous dogs. We stepped out onto the pavement. I got the flashlight out of the camper, and as we walked slowly toward Dad's truck Casey's hand slipped into mine. It felt good.

It was real quiet now. No traffic. Just the sound of Miss Tree's paws padding around and a little snuffling noise now and then as she inhaled some extra-interesting smell. That and a steady chorus of grasshoppers playing violins on their elbows.

I touched the hood of the truck. Cold. It had been here for a while. Slowly, I raised the light and shone it on the windshield. It reflected back in my eyes, leaving the inside of the truck in darkness. I reached for the door handle. It would be locked . . .

The latch clicked and released. The door opened. I swung the light up and shone it across the seat. Except for a crumpled potato chip bag and an empty styrofoam cup, the cab was empty. That's when I noticed I'd been holding my breath. I let it out in a long sigh of relief. "So far, so good," I said.

Casey nodded. "Yeah, but there's still the trailer." We walked around to the back. I handed Casey the light while I undid the latches.

"Okay, stand back," I said, and flung open the

back door. Except for the lingering smell left behind by the busy bowels of three big bulls, the trailer was empty. I shut the door.

"All right!" Casey said. "Your Dad's okay."

"Yeah? How you figure that? All we know is nobody murdered him and left his body in the truck. It's a big jump from there to okay. If he's okay where is he? And why'd he leave the truck here?"

Casey thought a minute. "That's pretty simple. The truck broke down. He left it here and hitched a ride to the next town and he's waiting to get the repairs for it."

"There's one way to find out." I walked back to the other truck and got the keys out of the ignition, then slid behind the wheel of the abandoned Chev. Casey looked at me like I'd lost the remainder of my mind. "Dad always keeps his spare keys on the other truck's key ring." I explained. "That way he never has to check on which set he needs." I could have added that it had been real useful for a guy who used to spend half his time so drunk he could barely find the truck, never mind the keys. I turned the key in the ignition. The engine turned over and started humming like a hive of healthy bees. I looked at Casey. "Any more theories, Sherlock?"

She shrugged. "At least I *had* a theory. You got any better ideas?"

"I wish I did." I shut off the truck, got out, and

walked in an aimless circle around it shining the light on the ground as if I expected to find *Hi, Shane, I went to town. Be back soon* painted in big white letters on the pavement. No such luck. But as I swung the light through the deep shadows between the front of the truck and the cottonwood tree I thought I caught the gleam of something shiny. I focused the light on it. An aluminum can. I reached under the tree and picked it up and read the familiar label — Lone Star beer. Yeah, that had been an old family favorite of our Montana days. My hand brushed something else. Cardboard. I dragged out a whole case of Lone Star empties. Plus a couple of empty whiskey bottles. Jack Daniels. That had been a popular brand, too.

And all of a sudden a whole lot of pieces started clicking together. Dad had been planning to catch up to some old friends in Butte. What if he never got that far? What if he met them on the road and they all pulled in here for a big reunion and the booze started flowin' and the party just kept goin'? It had happened before more times than I could count. Dad had promised to quit drinking after each one. And he'd done it, too — until he met some of his old buddies. Just 'cause he'd been sober for almost a year didn't mean it couldn't happen again.

I muttered a few words that would've earned me a smack from Casey's mom, and kicked the box of empties as hard as I could. It flew across the pavement like a wounded airplane, spewing cans from its caved-in top and scattering them in shiny arcs through the darkness. The case came to rest against a lamppost and collapsed. Collapsed just like the dream of a normal life I'd had this past year. Collapsed and drowned in a sea of beer.

Chapter 13

The last can clattered across the asphalt and silence settled in behind it. Casey's voice, cool as the night air, cut through the quiet. "Feel better now?"

"Not really."

"You want to tell me what that was all about?"

"Yeah, I'll tell you what it's about, Case. It's about this whole stupid trip was a waste of time. It's about me bein' a real slow learner. It's about chasin' five hundred miles after my dad just to find out he's out partyin' with his friends and can't be bothered comin' home — if he happens to even remember he's got a home." Or a kid, I felt like adding. But I didn't. I already sounded like I was gonna start bawling, and when you're fifteen and talking to your girlfriend that doesn't make you feel real mature.

"I don't believe I'm hearing this. You find a case of empties and all of a sudden that's proof your dad just up and abandoned his truck in the middle of nowhere and went off on a big drunk? Give me a break, Shane."

"Casey, you don't understand . . ." I began, but my voice went funny again and I turned away to stand staring into the darkness.

"You bet I don't understand. I don't understand who appointed you judge and jury to decide your dad's guilty until proven innocent. And I don't understand how you could come all this way looking for him, and then when you're this close to finding him you just write him off like he doesn't even matter anymore."

Casey wasn't finished, but fortunately the dog had just come trotting back from another exploration and distracted her. "Hey, Miss Tree, what have you got there?" she asked, bending down for a closer look. "Put it down, Miss! Don't you know it's dangerous to go picking up scraps people leave lying around? Dogs get poisoned that way. Miss, put it *down!* What on earth. . . ? Shane, look at this."

"I don't want to look at some piece of crap the dog dug up," I said through my teeth.

"Even if it's a bear paw?"

"What?" Against my better judgement I turned around and shone the light on the smelly black thing

Casey was holding. It really *was* a bear paw, claws and all.

"This is really weird," Casey said. "How did a bear paw end up here?"

I shrugged. "Off a dead bear. There's probably a few bears around here. We're not all that far from Yellowstone. It's full of bears."

Casey wasn't buying it. "You're telling me a bear just wandered out of the park, followed the highway almost a hundred miles, and then laid down and died here?"

I shrugged. "Good a place as any to lie down and die." I wouldn't have minded doing it myself right about now.

But Casey wasn't about to let it go. She shone the light on the paw and bent down for a closer look. I shook my head. Only a girl raised by a veterinarian could get this interested in a half-rotten bear paw. "Look, Shane!" she said, holding it up for me to see, "This didn't just fall off the bear. It's been cut off. See the straight edge on it?"

I backed up a step to inhale some fresher air. "Okay, okay, so it's been cut off. What's that got to do with anything? You figure Dad met a bear here, they fought a duel and he managed to cut its paw off but it still ate him and wandered off into the sunset digesting the evidence? Get real, Case." I turned away and started walking toward the truck.

"Where do you think you're going?"

"Where do you think? Home. Come on. Unless you want to wait for the bear to come back for dessert."

Right about then, Casey got mad. Real mad. I could almost see the sparks flying off her in the dark when she let me have it with both barrels. "So that's it? You're giving up? We drive about five hundred miles on a wild goose chase and then when we finally get close to finding some answers you just up and quit. I never thought you were a quitter, Shane." Most of it she yelled at me. Except for that last sentence. It came out real soft, and penetrated real deep.

I didn't answer her. I was thinking, remembering the last time I'd been on the receiving end of that "quitter" lecture. It had been a long time ago, when I was just a little kid. And it had come from a girl then, too. My mom. Funny how some things stick in your mind. A lot of things Mom said are still so clear. Maybe it's because when you realize somone's never coming back you kind of freeze-dry every little memory about them . . .

I was about six years old and I was trying to lasso a fencepost. After at least twenty misses I was so mad I was ready to bawl so I marched off in a big pout — but I tripped over the rope and fell flat on my face. Next thing I knew I was looking at a pair of feet. They were attached to my mom and she was looking down at me with a big grin on her face. "Cowboys don't quit, Shane," was all she said. But I think it might have been the most important advice I ever got. And now I'd just got it again.

"Okay, Case," I finally said, "so we don't give up. What do you want to do? Head on down to Butte and see if we can crash the party, or what?"

Casey just shook her head kind of absentmind-edly like she'd already forgotten about me. "No," she said. "Not yet. There's gotta be something else around here. Some clue to what's really going on . . ." With Miss Tree following her, nose to the ground, Casey started a long, slow stalk around the parking area, shining the light on the ground, the fence, the picnic tables, you name it. Finally she got to the phone booth and stood there study-ing something.

"What'd you find now, Sherlock?" I asked im-patiently.

"Hmm, this is interesting," she said. "The phone book's open to Butte."

"Wow, that *is* pretty amazing," I said sarcasti-cally. "So what?"

She ignored me. "There's a number circled here. The Roaring Dragon. It's a Chinese restaurant. I wonder what that could mean."

I sighed. "It means that some truck driver

wanted chop suey for supper so he called ahead for takeout."

That explanation impressed her so much that she ripped the page right out of the book and stuffed into her pocket.

"You can't do that!"

"I just did. Come on, we can make Butte by morning."

Chapter 14

Butte. In the moonlight it stood spooky and unreal, like a science-fiction city on an unfriendly planet. Skeletons of old mining machines rose gaunt and ghostly against the sky. They guarded their ancient slag heaps against the city of radioactive spiders whose lights swarmed up the steep side of the butte that gave the place its name . . .

Whoa! I gave my head a shake. I really was tired when my imagination got this wild.

I'd dozed off a couple of times in the last hour and was a little worried that Casey might do the same — which wouldn't have mattered except for the fact that she was driving. But she swore she was wide awake. I guess having a cat sitting on your shoulder playing pounce-on-the-mouse in your hair does help keep you alert.

Now I stretched and yawned and sat up straight as Casey wheeled the truck onto a silent downtown street. "Hey," I said, "the rodeo grounds aren't in the middle of town, you know."

"Nope. But the address for the Roaring Dragon was right around here somewhere."

I groaned. "Aw, come on, Case, will you give it up? That restaurant doesn't have anything to do with anything."

"Maybe not. But it's not gonna hurt to drive by the place, is it?"

I muttered under my breath and closed my eyes again. Next thing I knew, Casey was shouting, "There it is!" I looked up just in time to come face-to-face with a peeling portrait of a real ugly green dragon blowing out a whole snootful of hot red flames. Casey had pulled into a parking spot right in front of the door.

"Thought you were just driving by," I said sourly.

"I was, but since there's a parking spot I thought I'd pull in. Come on, let's check it out."

The place was closed, naturally, since there isn't a lot of interest in Chinese food at four a.m. But as I took a closer look through the window, I decided there wouldn't be a whole lot of interest in the food in this place any time. It was a dump. The neon letters that spelled out the name had a few burnt-out sections so the sign read HE ROARI G RAGO . Inside, dusty plastic hanging plants drooped over dingy tables and chairs with black electrical-tape patches on their torn seats. The only things that made the place look like a Chinese greasy spoon instead of a regular greasy spoon were the bottles of soy sauce on every table — and the fish tank. Sitting just inside the window was this huge, scummy fish tank, full of these honkin' huge ugly fish cruising slowly back and forth like nuclear submarines. I wondered if they were part of the menu or the decorations. Either way, they didn't do a thing for my appetite.

"Wow!" Casey said softly. "Look at the size of those fish! Too bad the place is closed. We could've got The Prince a breakfast he'd never forget."

"Case," I said, "from the looks of this place, The Prince might *be* breakfast. Let's get out of here. It's gettin' light enough now I think I can find the rodeo grounds." I backed the truck out onto the street and then took a shortcut through an alley to get back the way we came.

"Hey," Casey said as we passed the back end of the Roaring Dragon. "That place must be more popular than we thought. It's got its own private refrigerator truck." I glanced over behind the restaurant, and sure enough, gleaming white against the shadows sat a big, shiny new semi with an insulated trailer. Across the side it said THE ROARING DRAGON at the top, and something in Chinese at the bottom, and in between was a picture of that same old dragon with the bad case of heartburn, roaring his head off.

I shook my head. "That's pretty dumb, investing that kind of money to supply a dive like that greasy little restaurant. They'll be broke in no time." I stopped thinking about dragons and concentrated on finding the turnoff to the rodeo grounds.

The grounds weren't hard to find. Dad and I had been here at least a couple of times that I could remember, so I went looking in the right direction from town. But as soon as we came in sight of the arena and grandstands I got a sinking feeling in my stomach. The place was as deserted as last year's wasp nest. A few cotton candy holders and rodeo programs blowing in the wind were the only proof there had even been a rodeo here this week. Those and the posters still fastened on the poles along the road. BUTTE PROFESSIONAL RODEO JUNE 29–30, they said. And today was July 2.

I let the truck roll to a stop outside the main gate, cut the engine, and sat staring at the emptiness. I felt like another piece of garbage, helpless and aimless, being tossed around by each passing gust of wind. We'd hit a dead end. Now what?

Casey finally broke the silence. "I'm sorry, Shane," she said softly. "I really thought we might find him here. Or at least find somebody who had seen him."

I took a deep breath. "Yeah, I'm sorry, too," I said, starting the truck.

I started to turn around but Casey stopped me. "Wait a minute," she said, looking out the side window. "There's someone parked over there."

"Where?"

"Way back behind the chutes. You can't see it from your side. I think it's a truck and camper." I leaned over to get a look out her window and saw what she was looking at. "Could be somebody left over from the rodeo," Casey added. "Let's go talk to them. They might have seen your dad."

I shrugged. "What have we got to lose?" We bounced across the rough ground and pulled up beside the truck. It was pretty beat-up looking. If it did belong to somebody who was following the rodeos it didn't look like it would follow too many more. Probably it was broken down now, which would explain the fact that it was still here when everyone else was long gone.

I left Casey minding the zoo in our truck and wandered up to the back door of the other camper. It looked deserted, but I pounded on the door just in case. There was a bellow from inside, "Aw right, aw right, I'm comin', you don't have to knock the door down!" And just then I caught a glimpse of the personalized back licence plate. It read YIP PEE. Suddenly I knew who had let out the bellow. Buck McCain, the second-biggest drunk on the rodeo circuit. Well actually, the biggest, now that Dad had retired.

I was just putting two and two together when the camper door burst open and Buck staggered into the pale daylight. "Whadya want?" he coughed, rubbing his bloodshot eyes.

"Josh Morgan," I said, the words coming out hard as nails. "Tell him his son's here to get him."

Chapter 15

Buck blinked, rubbed his eyes, and stared at me. "What?" he croaked.

"You heard me. Tell my dad the party's over."

Buck slowly stuffed his shirttail into his jeans and pushed his hair back out of his eyes. "*You're* Josh's boy? Shane?"

"Yeah. Somethin' wrong with that?"

Buck laughed at me. "Got a burr under your saddle, ain't ya?"

"You bet I have. Now will you just go throw some water on my old man and send him out here?"

"Sure," Buck said. "I'd get a real bang outta that. Trouble is, I ain't seen your dad for almost a year."

That knocked the wind out of me like a punch in the stomach. "You mean he's not here?" I said.

"That's probably why I ain't seen him."

I was beginning to feel like the biggest fool in the U.S.A. "He never showed up at the rodeo here at all?"

"Shane," Buck said slowly. "The last time I ran into your dad was last August, up at Missoula. He was bull fightin' at the rodeo there. I invited him over to my outfit that night and got out the bottle just like I always did when me and Josh got together. But he wouldn't touch a drop. Told me the booze had almost cost him the only thing he had left in the world that mattered to him." Buck's bleary eyes met mine with a steady look that I couldn't face. "He was talkin' about you, Shane," he said, as I studied a tear in the leg of my jeans. "He said he was never goin' back to drinkin'. I think he meant it, Shane."

He paused and a long silence grew between us. I didn't know what to say. Finally, Buck spoke again. "So what made you think he was here?"

I told him the whole story, wishing all the while that I could just crawl in a hole and disappear. It doesn't feel real good to find out that a hopeless drunk has more faith in your dad than you do.

After I finished, Buck rubbed a hand across the stubble on his jaw and then nodded. "You went through some pretty bad times with your dad after your mom was killed. I guess it takes a while to learn to trust again. But people do change, Shane. *Some* people. Wish I was one of 'em. I'm still tryin' to sober up from a party two nights ago," he added, with a grin that didn't hide the shame in his eyes. "But I do know for sure that none of the cowboys that came here to Butte had seen hide nor hair of your dad lately. His name came up when we were all sittin' around talkin' after the show. Everybody wondered how he was doin' but nobody seemed to know. So if the fella back in Bozeman said Josh was headin' here for the rodeo and you found his truck along the way, somethin' pretty serious must've happened."

"Yeah, I guess you're right," I said. My throat had suddenly gone so dry I could hardly talk. "Uh, thanks, Buck. Sorry I came roarin' in here with a big chip on my shoulder and started yellin' at you like that."

Buck shrugged. "Don't let it worry you none, kid. Everybody else yells at me." I turned to go but Buck stopped me. "Shane?" I looked back at him. "Good luck findin' him."

I swallowed hard, but the lump in my throat wouldn't go away, so I just nodded. I had a real bad feeling that I was going to need all the luck I could get.

Back in the truck I told Casey what Buck had said. She listened in silence, only her eyes showing that she understood as well as I did just how serious things were now. When I finished she put into words what I'd been thinking. "We've got to tell the police now," she said softly.

I nodded. "Should have told them a long time ago," I said miserably. "He's probably dead by now."

Casey reached out and laid a firm hand on my arm. "Don't, Shane," she said.

I buried my face in my hands. "I'm sorry," I said. "It's just that . . ."

"I know," she said. "But there could be a lot of explanations of where he is. Dead is the last one we're gonna believe. Okay?"

I nodded. "Okay."

"Good. Then let's go find a phone booth so we can call the police."

I shook my head. "No. It's too complicated to tell over the phone. They'll want to talk to us in person anyway. I'm pretty sure I saw a cop station when we were driving around downtown. Let's go back and find it."

Ten minutes later we were cruising slowly around downtown again — right past the good old Roaring Dragon. Even though it was only 6:15, the place seemed to have opened up for the day. At least, all the lights were on inside and a couple of cars were parked out front. I took a second look at the cars. One was a white Lincoln. The other was a

BMW. Not exactly the class of customer I would have expected at a place as grungy as this. Then I noticed the three mud-streaked four-by-fours with horse trailers behind them, parallel parked across the street. None of those vehicles had been here when we checked the place before, and since nothing else in sight was open I figured all the drivers must be in having breakfast. Next thing I knew I was wheeling the Ford in alongside the Lincoln.

Casey shot me a startled look. I shrugged. "Looks like this is where everybody in town comes for breakfast. We might as well grab something to eat before we find the police station."

"Thought you wouldn't eat in this place to save your life."

"Well, they can't do much to toast and coffee," I said, wondering if Casey could see past the excuses to the fact that I'd do anything to postpone the moment I had to report my dad missing to the police.

"Only one way to find the answer to that," she said, starting to get out. I got out, too, but before I could shut the door Miss Tree went into one of her whining fits.

I sighed. "Remind me never to take a small-bladdered dog on a trip across Montana again," I said, letting the dog out. "I'll take her back in the alley. Maybe you should put The Prince in the camper so he doesn't try to jump out when we open the doors again."

Miss and I headed around the corner. She did what she had to do while I stood gazing at the sunrise, pretending she wasn't my dog. The next time I took my eyes off the sky she had disappeared. I swung around and scanned the restaurant's back lot. I couldn't see the dog. But then I heard her whining and scratching at something. The sound led me around to the back of the shiny white Roaring Dragon refrigerator truck. Miss was up on her hind legs scratching at the door of the trailer. I caught her by the scruff of the neck. "Forget it, Miss Tree. No matter how much you complain I ain't about to buy you a truckload of sweet and sour spare ribs. Now come on." Reluctantly, looking back over her shoulder every step of the way, she let me lead her back to our truck.

I opened the door cautiously, just in case that four-legged, fur-covered tornado hit me in mid-air, but the cab was empty. For once Casey must have taken my advice. I shut the dog in and walked over to where Casey was waiting by the restaurant door. We went inside.

With all the vehicles parked out there I was surprised to see that only one table, near the back, was occupied. I was even more surprised at the combination of people who were sitting together there. Two of them were Chinese. They were both wearing suits. And, although suits aren't something I know a lot about, I would have bet the ones these guys were wearing cost big bucks. I mentally assigned the suits to the Lincoln and the BMW.

The other three definitely belonged in the four-by-fours. "Wild and furry and full of fleas and never been curried below the knees." That was a line Dad always used to describe guys like these. One wore a beat-up black hat jammed down over long, greasy hair, a buckskin jacket stained almost black with dirt and grease, torn jeans, and a big hunting knife in a sheath at his belt. The other two had on baseball caps, greasy jeans, and jean jackets. One wore heavy, steel-toed workboots and the other had on tall, mud-caked rubber boots. All three of them looked like they'd be real startled to meet up with a bar of soap.

What those three hillbillies had to discuss with the two guys who looked like they might own most of Hong Kong was more than I could figure out. But whatever it was, they were all sitting around that table with their heads together like they were planning the deal of the century.

But before I could wonder about it any more, my train of thought got derailed by some guy in a grubby white jacket. He must have been a waiter, or maybe the cook, but whoever he was, he didn't have much of a way with customers. He came out of the kitchen waving a dish towel at us and yelling something in Chinese. I guess it finally occurred to him that we didn't speak the language because he switched to English. "Out! Out! Go away! Not open! You go now!"

Well, my first impression of this joint had been bad and nothing had happened to improve it any, so it shouldn't have been hard to convince me to leave. But something in this guy's attitude hit me all wrong. I don't like being shooed out of public places like a chicken that's wandered into the living room. "The door was open," I said.

That didn't do much to calm him down. He waved his arms around some more. "Mistake. Forgot to lock. Not open for customers yet. You go now." He had taken me by the arm and was pushing me toward the door.

I shook loose. "Yeah? Well if you're not open, what about them?" I jerked my head toward the table at the back. "What's the matter, don't we fit the dress code? What is it anyhow? Suits or slobs and nothin' in between?"

"Shane, cool it," Casey whispered.

By this time the cook-waiter-bouncer was getting annoyed. He grabbed my arm again and threw me against a table so hard the bottle of soy sauce hit the floor and broke with a sound like a rifle shot.

I bounced off a chair and ended up sprawled across the table. Half-stunned, it took me a minute to shake the cobwebs out of my head, but by that time the situation was out of my hands. Casey had taken over.

She was standing eyeball to eyeball with Mr. White Jacket yelling at him at the top of her voice. "You leave Shane alone. Touch him again and I'll have the cops here so fast it'll make your moustache spin."

I don't know if White Jacket was impressed, but she sure did get the attention of the gents at the back table. Next thing I knew the older one of the "suits" was picking me up, dusting me off, and mumbling apologies in several languages. Then he turned on White Jacket and ran up and down him in angry Chinese until the guy looked about ready to melt into the floor.

Turning back to me, Mr. Suit apologized again, in English, with a British accent. "Please, you must forgive my employee's rudeness. He is an ignorant young man. Of course, if the door was open you had every right to come in. Please," he oozed, smooth as a used-car salesman, "sit. Make yourself comfortable." He steered us in the direction of a table in better shape than the one I'd landed on. "Here, take a menu. Order whatever you like for breakfast. It's — what is your expression? — on the house."

I hesitated for a minute trying to take in just exactly what was going on here. Why did White Jacket want us out so bad? And why had his boss rushed in like the Lone Ranger to rescue us from White Jacket? Then I remembered what Casey had been yelling at White Jacket. So what was there about the word "cops" that rang Mr. Suit's alarm clock?

I decided that breakfast might be a real interesting idea. "Okay," I said slowly, throwing a dirty look over my shoulder at White Jacket. "We'll take you up on that offer." I flashed Casey a "just do it" look before she could argue. We sat down. Mr. Suit nodded and smiled at us one more time, gave White Jacket an earful of stern instructions, and headed back to rejoin his little club.

Casey leaned across the table. "Shane," she said in a fierce whisper, "are you out of your mind? An hour ago you wouldn't have eaten here if you were starving to death. Now the friendly waiter practically breaks your neck, and you decide to stay for breakfast?"

"There's somethin' weird goin' on here," I muttered from behind my menu. "This restaurant business is just a front for somethin' illegal. And I'd bet my bottom dollar that little get-together in the back corner's part of it."

Casey grinned. "You better hang on to your bottom

dollar. It's one of the few we've got left." Then she turned serious. "Are you beginning to believe what I said about that circled phone number being related to your dad going missing?"

I shook my head. "I don't know, Case. I just don't know what's goin' on anymore."

Right then Mr. White Jacket strolled by. He walked up to the front door and locked it.

Chapter 16

This was not good news. Casey had her back to the door and didn't see White Jacket lock it, but the look on my face must have telegraphed trouble.

"Shane? What's going on?" she whispered.

"Don't turn around. The waiter just — " At that moment White Jacket strode up to our table. I gulped and rearranged my sentence. "The waiter, uh, just wants to take our order now. I'll have the ham and eggs and pancakes. How about you, Casey?"

Not being a slow learner, Casey gave the scowling waiter a big smile and said, "Make that two, please." He growled some sort of reply, snatched the menus and disappeared into the kitchen.

When I was sure he was gone I told Casey, "He

just locked the front door. You think we should throw a chair through the window and split while we've got the chance?"

Casey thought a minute. Then she shook her head. "No, I'd guess he's just making sure they don't get any more unwanted customers. The boss is playing it cool, I think. He wants us to eat our free breakfasts and go away. He's not really worried about us. Probably thinks we're just a couple of stupid kids."

"Well, he's got that right," I said.

We sat there in silence for a while, waiting for breakfast. All of a sudden Casey grabbed the front of her jacket and let out a muffled squawk. I thought she was about to have a heart attack — until she unzipped the jacket and The Prince stuck his head out.

Then *I* just about had a heart attack. "Casey! What do you think you're doin' with that cat in here? When the waiter finds out he'll blow his cork."

"Well, if you quit making such a commotion about it he won't find out. The Prince is hungry. Settle down, Princey," she said in a much friendlier tone. "Breakfast is on its way."

She was right about that. The next second the kitchen door opened. "Ditch the cat," I hissed. "Here he comes."

Casey unceremoniously stuffed the insulted Prince's head back out of sight and zipped her jacket to her chin. I wondered if White Jacket noticed that Casey's chest was heaving like she'd just run a marathon, as he slammed the plates on the table and sulked back off toward the kitchen again.

The food wasn't great but we got rid of it — fast.

The three of us, that is. Casey took two bites for herself and then slipped a tidbit of ham inside her jacket. It disappeared instantly. Once she slipped up and took three bites before remembering to share. "Merrow?" said Casey's chest in a voice that seemed to fill the quiet of the almost-empty restaurant. Instantly Casey broke out in a coughing fit, cleared her throat, and said loudly, "Oh, man, is my throat ever getting sore. Did you hear me croak when I tried to talk just then?"

I shoved a big forkful of pancake in my mouth before I could burst out laughing. Casey remembered her manners and shared properly from then on. I remembered mine and wrapped a chunk of stringy ham in a napkin and stuffed it in my pocket. Once Miss Tree smelled ham on that cat's breath there'd be hell to pay if she didn't get some, too.

We were just about finished when Casey took a cautious glance around, opened her jacket, and brought out The Prince. The next thing I knew she had set him in my arms. "Quick, put him inside your jacket. I've got to go to the bathroom." Then she strolled off and I was left holding the cat.

I had just hidden The Prince from sight when I heard Casey gasp, "Oh, no!" I turned around in time to see her down on the floor starting to pick up all the stuff that had fallen out of her knapsack, which she had somehow managed to turn upside down just after she passed the guys at the back table.

There was junk all over the place. Coins rolled in all directions, a roll of Life Savers, more pens and pencils than I'd owned in my entire school career, makeup, a notebook . . . And it was taking her forever to pick it all up. So long that all five of the men had stopped talking and were now staring at her.

Casey, get out of there! I was thinking so hard that it must have finally worked. She gathered up the last stray penny, and happy as if she was in her right mind, strolled on around the corner to the bathroom. A minute later Mr. Suit stood up and said something I couldn't hear to the others, and they all disappeared out a door in the opposite corner. I breathed a sigh of relief. We still hadn't found out what was going on but at least we weren't in any real trouble — yet.

Casey finally came sauntering back. I jumped up, startling The Prince so he dug his claws into my stomach, and started for the door. "Come on," I told Casey, "we're gettin' out of here."

"Where'd they all go?" she asked, glancing back at the empty table.

"Out the back door. And we're goin' out the front while we still can."

"Don't you think we should leave a tip for you-know-who?" she asked, straight-faced. But she headed for the door. Getting out was as simple as turning the handle on the lock. I caught a glimpse of White Jacket watching us from the kitchen door, but he didn't make a move.

I breathed a sigh of relief as the door closed behind us. "Well, that was educational," Casey said.

"Yeah? All I learned was not to cross the waiter," I said, massaging a bruise on my ribs where I'd hit the table.

"But you didn't spill your knapsack right behind those guys' table, did you?"

I turned to stare at her. "You did that on purpose?"

"You didn't think I was naturally that clumsy, did you?"

It was safer to ask another question than to answer that one. "So what did you hear?"

"Not enough to really tell me anything, but enough to make me real curious about just what *is* going on."

"Well?" I asked impatiently.

"It's just bits and pieces. Two of the grungy mountain men just came from Yellowstone, I think. The other one had driven down from Glacier Park overnight."

That didn't make any sense. "But what business would three half-tame hillbillies like them have with a couple of rich Chinese guys in a rundown restaurant in Butte?"

Casey shrugged. "Beats me, but I'm sure they've got some kind of a deal going. They also said something about it being good that they'd unloaded the trailers before daylight."

A bunch of stock trailers being unloaded before daylight at a restaurant? Were these guys rustling cattle and selling them to the Roaring Dragon? Sure, they just rounded them up, loaded them in the trailer and chased them straight into the kitchen. Talk about getting your meat *fresh*.

No, that idea wouldn't fly. But what *could* they have had in those trailers that they'd unload here? "Did they say anything else?" I asked Casey.

"Not really. About that time they noticed me and shut up. Oh, wait a minute. There was one other thing. Something about another package. One of them said something about how it should soon have cooled off enough not to be dangerous, and they all laughed."

I shook my head. Now I was beginning to imagine some really weird stuff. Something that had been hot and dangerous? Were we into something really big-time here? Like smuggling uranium into China to make nuclear weapons? I thought China already had nuclear weapons. But the big question was, what did all this have to do with Dad? Probably nothing. I still figured the phone number at the roadside rest stop where we found Dad's truck was just a coincidence. Wasn't it?

One thing was for sure, though. We couldn't sort this out on our own. "Here, take your sharp-toenailed little friend," I said to Casey, taking The Prince out of my jacket. "I'm gonna take a quick look at those trailers and then we're going to the police station."

I ran across the deserted early-morning street, dodged behind the closest trailer, and came out alongside the far side of it. If anyone was watching from the restaurant they couldn't see me now. I walked the length of all three trucks and trailers. Nothing too unusual about any of them. Muddy and beat up as though they'd been through some real rough country. All three trucks had gun racks behind the seats and big rifles in each rack. But that wasn't real surprising. Half the four-by-fours in Alberta had gun racks in them, and Americans had a reputation for being even more attached to their guns.

But there was something about the trailers that bothered me. I couldn't figure out what it was. I couldn't see inside without opening the back doors, and I thought that might look a little obvious, but as I walked along the outside of them something didn't seem right.

Suddenly, I knew what it was. The smell. Any livestock trailer as dirty as these were on the outside wasn't likely to have been cleaned inside for a while either. They should smell like livestock had been in there. In other words, like manure — and lots of it. I remembered how the smell had come right out of Dad's trailer and hit me like a freight train. But these trailers didn't smell. At least not that way. But there *was* a smell. A kind of sweet, metallic smell. I looked down at the crack under the back door. Something dark and gummy was caked on the dark brown paint. I reached out and touched it. My hand came away sticky and stained dark red. There was blood smeared all over the back of the trailer.

I felt the hair on the back of my neck prickle. What was going on here? We had to talk to the cops. Fast. I came around the end of the trailer just in time to see Casey open the truck door.

Then everything happened at once. Miss Tree shot out of the truck like a cork out of a champagne bottle. The Prince exploded out of Casey's arms and went tearing around the side of the Roaring Dragon with the dog in hot pursuit. Casey took off after the two of them.

"Casey, wait!" I yelled, but she didn't hear me. I

started across the street, but there was a sudden blast of a horn, and I stopped just in time to avoid getting run over by a garbage truck.

By the time I got across the street and around the corner Casey was nowhere in sight.

Chapter 17

I couldn't see Casey or The Prince. But there was Miss Tree, scratching at the back door of that refrigerator truck again.

I'd started over to get her when I heard a low whistle behind me. I spun around but I couldn't see where it was coming from. Then, a loud whisper, "Shane, down here." Casey was flat on the ground behind a pile of old boxes along the side of the building.

"Casey, are you ... " I began, but she stopped me with a loud "*shhh!*" She waved at me to come over. I noticed that she hadn't caught the cat, but I didn't think that was what she wanted to tell me. I came up next to her and she motioned me down on the ground.

I crouched beside her and finally caught on to what she was doing. From this angle you could see through a dirty little window into the basement. The five men were down there. They were all leaning over a briefcase that was open on the table. The Chinese guy who hadn't talked to us was taking something out of the briefcase and handing it to the three greasy guys. It was money. Big stacks of money. They were all looking real happy. I could hear them laughing.

"Well it went pretty smooth, didn't it, Tom?" one of the hillbillies said to the other.

"Yeah, but it would have been even smoother if you hadn't gone and got drunk and met up with the wrong truck and trailer."

The wrong truck and trailer? Casey and I exchanged glances, reading each other's minds. The first guy was talking again. "Yeah, but it'll work out okay. Nobody'll ever suspect." He bent over and started stuffing his share of the money into a gym bag and I couldn't hear what he said next. As he straightened up I caught the end of his sentence, ". . . cowboy happened to freeze to death in the middle of summer." He laughed and slapped his buddy on the back as if it was the joke of the century.

I turned ice cold, because I'd suddenly realized something that scared me to death. I jumped to my feet and dragged Casey with me. "Go to that pay phone at the end of the block. Tell the cops to get here fast!" I threw the words over my shoulder as I ran for the truck.

Seconds later I was running back through the alley with the tire iron in my hand. Miss Tree was still there, pawing at the door of the refrigerator truck. "Look out, Miss," I panted. "I get the message. I just hope it's not too late."

I jammed the end of the iron in the crack between the door and the wall and pried. Nothing happened. That door was solid as a rock. I moved the tire iron a little lower, took a deep breath, and leaned on it with every ounce of strength I had. I felt something give a little. I moved it and tried again. Still not enough to break the latch. One more try. Every muscle in my body ached with the strain, but I couldn't budge it.

And then, all of a sudden, I felt an extra surge of power. I looked over my shoulder. Casey was back, leaning on the tire iron with all her strength, too. There was a sudden screech of wounded metal and the door sagged open. A cloud of ice fog billowed out into the early-morning sunshine. It cleared and I got my first look inside.

I couldn't believe what I was seeing. Beside me, Casey gasped. For a few seconds neither of us said anything. We just stared. The sight was enough to make you sick. Animal heads. Dozens of them stared at us through dead, glazed eyes. Mountain sheep with huge, curling horns, trophy bull moose, six-point white-tail bucks, cougars, black bears, grizzly bears. In another corner there was a huge pile of elk antlers, still in velvet, hacked raggedly from the skulls. And hides. Piles and piles of fresh hides. Lynx, wolf, bear. Near the front was a stack of something black. It took a minute for my eyes to adjust to the dimness enough to recognize what I was looking at. Bear paws. Dozens of bear paws. Just like the paw Miss Tree had found back at Dad's truck.

But right in front of us was the spookiest sight of all. Jars. Just regular jam jars. At least twenty of them. And inside each one was this lumpy little organ of some sort. Casey reached out and picked up one of the jars. "Gall bladders," she said in this kind of awe-struck voice. For a minute I thought she meant human ones and I just about lost all that free ham and eggs and pancakes right then and there. "Bear gall bladders," she explained. "There was an article about them in the paper Mom gets from the World Wildlife Fund. In Asia people believe they have magic healing powers. They're worth thousands of dollars each." She shifted her gaze to the bear paws. "And those are a delicacy in fancy restaurants there. I remember reading that some people pay 1,400 dollars a plate for them."

I couldn't do anything but stand there staring unbelieving at the mutilated remains of at least a hundred beautiful wild animals. Miss Tree had pushed in past us and was sniffing at the hides. I should stop her.

"Shane," Casey's voice broke into my thoughts. "Do you realize what we've stumbled into here?"

"Yeah, I think so," I said, my voice coming out in a near-whisper, "but I still can't believe it." I still felt half-stunned by what I was seeing — and worried sick by what I wasn't seeing. Dad. Where was he?

What those guys had said about meeting the wrong truck and trailer and about the cowboy freezing to death all added up to one thing. Somehow they had managed to kidnap Dad and lock him in here. But he wasn't here. Did that mean he was already dead and dumped somewhere in the desert? Had I trailed him this far just to get here too late?

Miss Tree's excited whining broke the silence. She had her nose right under the hides now, rooting like a nosey pig. The pile shifted and some top ones slid off, leaving a cowboy boot sticking out. I bent down and started dragging hides in all directions. He was huddled under half a dozen bearskins, pale and cold and silent.

"Dad!" I screamed, the word echoing in the icy air. "No!"

Chapter 18

He blinked. Then his eyes focused on me. His blue lips curled into a grin. "Hey, Shane!" he croaked through chattering teeth. "Guess I haven't died and gone to heaven if you're here. 'Bout time you showed up. This is one heck of a cold place to spend the night, even if they do give you lots of bedding."

I sank down beside him and wrapped my arms around him. "Dad." My voice choked up on me and for a minute I couldn't say another word. But I didn't need to because Dad reached his ice-cold arms around me and hugged me half to death. I didn't know anybody that cold could make you feel so warm inside.

There was a loud shout from somewhere outside and then a string of angry, rapid-fire Chinese. I spun around to look through the door in time to see all five of our friends from the restaurant come pounding across the back lot toward us. Both Chinese guys had guns in their hands.

We were trapped, sitting ducks with nowhere to run, and I figured that in about five seconds we were doomed to join the rest of the dead meat in this truck. But I didn't figure on the lightning reflexes of Casey Sutherland. Before I could even stand up she had swung around and slammed the door with all her strength. To my total amazement that warped latch caught and held. The door sagged drunkenly but it was solid as a rock.

"There!" Casey announced proudly, "that'll hold 'em till the cops get here." Then the roar of the engine vibrated through the floor beneath us and with a screech of tires the truck lurched forward. In the sudden pitch darkness I heard Casey gulp and say, "Uh-oh!"

That pretty well said it all. In the next second the truck swerved wildly, dumping Casey on top of us and shattering a couple of gall bladder jars. Miss Tree gave a startled yelp and skidded over to start worriedly licking any face she could find. Then the truck straightened out and started gaining speed.

The next few minutes were totally unreal. In the mid-winter cold we rocketed, blind and freezing, through the steep streets of Butte, squealing our way around corners, seeming to fly off the tops of hills, then feeling the jolt of the tortured springs as we hit the road again and began the wild plunge downhill. I remembered a ride on the midway at the Calgary Stampede. It had been called the North Pole. It hadn't been any big deal. But *this* was definitely a ride that deserved the name.

It was hard to believe but we were gaining even more speed. I figured we must be out of the city and ripping through the countryside. Where were they taking us? Had the cops even seen us? What if they hadn't? How long would we last in here if these guys got away and just kept heading for Seattle or some-place even farther away? I held Dad's icy body closer, trying to share what little warmth I still had with him. My other arm reached out for Casey, Miss Tree squeezed in, and the four of us huddled to-gether, a tiny island of life surrounded by frozen death.

I don't know how long we drove. It seemed like the road was all curves and I wondered how many more the screaming tires could handle. The answer came all too soon. We twisted sharply to the left and there was a sudden jolt. The truck was all over the road. "Hang on!" Dad yelled, tightening his grip on both Casey and me. The next thing I knew it felt like we were sailing through the air. Then we crashed.

For a minute there I didn't know if I was alive or dead. But then I realized that, aside from being buried in bearskins, I seemed to be okay. Miss Tree was already busy investigating all the corners of the truck and I could see Dad and Casey slowly untangling themselves, too. Wait a second — I could *see*. The crash had finished off the already-sprung door and sunlight was pouring in, mixing with the cold air and forming a dense cloud of fog. "Hey," I began, "let's get outta . . . "

There was a click. A real ominous click. I had a bad feeling I might know what made a click like that but I had to squint through the fog to make sure. I was right. It was a rifle being cocked. A thirty-thirty to be exact. It was in the hands of the ugliest of the three greasy hillbillies and the barrel was moving slowly back and forth to take in all three of us so nobody would feel left out.

"Well, Tom," he said over his shoulder. "Looks like we'll have to get rid of these two nosey kids, too."

He stepped up into the trailer, still keeping us all covered with the rifle. "Okay, just step back there, little girl. You too, kid. And don't you even think about movin', cowboy." Out of the corner of his eye he caught a glimpse of Miss Tree. She had discovered the mother lode of those tasty bear paws she'd had a sample of last night, and she was gnawing away for all she was worth. "Hey, you mangy hound! Drop that!" He aimed a kick in her direction.

That may have been the biggest mistake of his life. Miss Tree dropped the paw all right but the kick never connected because she went for his leg. I'd never seen so many teeth in one place before. Mr. Ugly gave a squawk, the rifle barrel wavered, and I dove in and hit him in the flabby belly with my head. The shot nearly deafened me, but the bullet screamed harmlessly through the roof. Before he could fire again Casey had smashed a gall bladder jar over his head. He sagged and I pushed him back out the door.

Right about then the whole area got real full of sirens. I pulled the door shut again just as Miss Tree threw back her head and started singing along.

A few cool seconds later a voice boomed out through a bullhorn. "Whoever's inside that trailer come out with your hands up! This is the police." We did. Except for Miss Tree, who came out with a bear paw in her mouth.

Not too surprisingly, it turned out that the Gall Bladder Gang wasn't half as brave facing humans who also had guns as they were at blowing away helpless animals. The one who had been driving the truck was still out cold from the crash and the others, who'd been following in the BMW, were all rounded up without firing a shot.

147

An hour later we had finally made it to Butte police headquarters and were sitting there eating doughnuts and patching together the whole story. They had wanted to take Dad to the hospital, but being Dad, he laughed at that idea and settled instead for sitting in the sunshine, wrapped in a blanket, and downing about a gallon of steaming coffee.

The police told us we'd just helped bust the biggest wildlife poaching ring that had ever operated in Montana. The police and the park rangers had known for a long time something like this was going on, but with Montana being such a big, wild place, they didn't have enough officers to catch the poachers. Now they not only had the poachers, but the money and brains of the operation, too. Ho Lem was his name and he had an exporting business out of Seattle. They trucked the animal parts to his warehouse there, and he shipped them out to Hong Kong under the cover of a legal business.

Dad listened as the detective explained it all. Then he laughed. "Yeah, I'm not surprised the brains of the outfit wasn't one of those poachers I first met up with. Put together, those three would be lucky to have the IQ of the three bulls I hauled down here.

"I'd just pulled off onto a rest stop west of Bozeman to check a low tire when this gorilla comes staggering over to my truck, drunk as a skunk, and tries to give me a drink of whiskey. Well," he went on, giving me a wink, "as Shane knows, I don't do that anymore, so I politely refused. Then this guy starts goin' on about how many gall bladders he's got." Dad shook his head. "I thought I'd run up against somethin' kinky enough to hit the *National Enquirer*. But then he showed me inside his trailer. To make a long story short, when I saw what he was up to I punched him in the jaw, tied him up with a bull halter, and was about to haul him off to the nearest police station when another truck pulled in. I went over to ask whoever it was to keep an eye on the trailer full of evidence for me till I could get the police." Dad grinned and took another swallow of coffee. "Too bad that guy turned out to be the first one's partner, pullin' in with another load of animal parts. He aimed a rifle at my head and convinced me to change my plans."

The detective went on to explain about how a conservation organization had offered a reward for catching anybody involved in trafficking in wild animal parts, and that we had a thousand dollars coming to us. But we all agreed we'd take enough to buy gas home and give the rest back so they could catch some more of these slimy killers. He also said we were all heroes. Including Miss Tree, who grinned up at him and accepted her fourth doughnut.

Dad laid a hand on my shoulder. "I just couldn't believe it when I opened my eyes and saw you there," he said. "I figured I was all out of luck and nobody would ever have the faintest clue what had happened to me when they found me on some back road, frozen solid. I don't know how you tracked me all the way from home to Butte with nothin' to go on. What kept you goin' anyhow?"

Casey and I exchanged grins. "Didn't Mom ever tell you, Dad? Cowboys don't quit."

A little while later the police drove us back to the restaurant to get our truck. Dad and Miss Tree rode up front with the officer. Casey and I were alone in the back. It was the first chance I'd had to talk to her alone since everything had started happening so fast this morning.

"Case," I said. "You're the one that kept me goin'. I was ready to give up a dozen times. If it hadn't been for you we never would've found Dad. What can I say?"

She grinned. "Don't say anything." So, I didn't. I leaned over and kissed her instead. It was the first time I'd ever kissed a girl in the back of a police car. It was so nice I'm thinking of taking up a life of crime just so I can do it again soon.

Then, as we were pulling up beside our truck, something else hit me. "Case, I'm real sorry we couldn't find The Prince." We'd searched all around the back lot of the Roaring Dragon before we went to the police station but we didn't find a whisker.

Casey swallowed. "I know," she said, "you tried. But after all that commotion there was no way he'd still be around. I just hope somebody finds him and looks after him."

The officer let us all out and we said goodbye and started to get into our truck. But Miss Tree started whining. I groaned. "Not again, Miss." Wearily, I took her around behind the building. "Hurry up. Get it over with." But next thing I knew she had trotted over and was peering into a narrow crack between the building and a Dumpster. Her ears were pricked up and her tail was wagging.

She stuck her nose into the crack. There was an explosive hiss and Miss Tree yelped and recoiled out of there licking a brand new scratch on her black rubber nose.